Hussies

Nathalie Gray
Ciana Stone
Sally Painter

ELLORA'S CAVE
ROMANTICA®
ELLORASCAVE.COM

CASSIOPEIA
Nathalie Gray

In the cutthroat world of space couriers, can a woman trust her heart to a competitor?

He's big. He's bad. And badass Ty Weller is sex on legs as far as rival Jackie Clark is concerned. She's been looking from a distance for years, wanting to touch, hungry for the kind of things she knows Ty can do with that dirty mouth. But something always got in the way—deadlines, rivalry, distance. Not this time. She'll get a taste if it's the last thing she does.

When Ty wants something, he takes it. He's had it in for the little motormouth since day one and intends to conquer that too. What he didn't expect was that he may have to give his heart in return.

SIN IN JEANS
Ciana Stone

Sin in jeans. If ever a cowboy fit that description, it's Tyler Austin. 'Cept this is no "boy". Ty's all man, and sexy as sin from his gorgeous eyes to his large...feet. To hell with the business Dale's in town for—she's itching to ride him from the moment she claps eyes on him.

Dale's past the age of quick flings or one-night stands, but the rugged cowboy has Dale two-stepping a mind change quicker than a gal can say "let's ride". And ride her he does—all night long.

But Dale's there to see a man about a horse. Getting sidetracked by this hunky cowboy is only temporary. Until fate throws them together—in more ways than one.

FAE'S GARGOYLE
Sally Painter

Maria Jennings awakes to find a naked man in bed with her—how he got there is a blank. Her shock soon turns to panic when she recognizes gargoyle warrior Denton Prescott, the man she's loved—and hungered for—for years. Before she can steal away, Denton, the sexiest hunk ever to draw breath is seducing her again, and it's every bit as hot as she ever dreamed.

Scorching sex aside, Maria is a Hussy, and her reawakened desires for him threaten her mission—to save Denton. But Denton has a mission of his own—convincing Maria it takes more than the loss of gargoyle magic to stop two soul mates from falling in love. He'll use every weapon in his erotic arsenal to prove it.

An Ellora's Cave Publication

www.ellorascave.com

Hussies

ISBN 9781419969812
ALL RIGHTS RESERVED.
Cassiopeia Copyright © 2008 Natalie Gray
Sin in Jeans Copyright © 2008 Ciana Stone
Fae's Gargoyle Copyright © 2008 Sally Painter
Edited by Mary Moran and Sue-Ellen Gower.
Cover design by Syneca.
Cover photography by konradbak/fotolia.com.

Trade paperback publication 2013

HUSSIES

ဢ

CASSIOPEIA
Nathalie Gray

ဆာ

Acknowledgements

∞

Thank you to the four other Hussies authors—Nicole Austin, Sahara Kelly, Sally Painter and Ciana Stone—and to Da Dude S.L. Carpenter, for providing laughs, chocolate-covered mint cookies, insight, joy, pizza, wisdom and hugs. Your collective goodness makes writing a fun and irreverent adventure. I love you—no, not in *that* way!

Prologue

ဢ

Myth, magic or legend? There have been Hussies since before time was measured in days and minutes. Women who fought bravely alongside their mates with sword and axe, warriors whose courage changed the world around them. Led by the first Hussy, Danu, these fierce fighters discovered their inner strengths, summoned reserves they didn't know they possessed and passed into the fabric of legend with their daring exploits.

Since that time, myths have been spun around the Hussy Warriors—tales told by firelight, whispered from mother to daughter—eventually to take their place amongst the mystical fables that shape our souls.

But the essence of a Hussy remains strong in the hearts of so many women. Heroines who don't realize that within them lies the power to make a difference, to effect change, to use their passion every bit as skillfully as Danu wielded her sword so long ago. Warriors in different times and different places, who love as deeply and desire as desperately as any woman ever has, seldom knowing that their desire will impact not just one man, but so much more.

Therein lies the magic of a Hussy. To right a wrong, turn a frown to a smile—to positively change those around her. To love a man with every fiber of her body, to learn from that love and to grow stronger because of it.

Whether in the past, the future or the here-and-now, there are Hussies around each corner. They may not even be aware of their Hussy destiny. But one thing is certain—when passion knocks on their door, lives will change for the better. And when it comes to their one special hero? Well, he's in for the ride of his life.

Which leaves one unanswered question...are *you* a Hussy?

Chapter One

❧

Alarms buzzed like swarms of insects. She ignored them just as she did the array of blinking lights telling her to either slow down or risk losing the ship and its intelligence data. To her right, the nav console on the clunky old cruiser winked a few times as if trying to warn her contact was imminent, giving her a few precious seconds to lock her elbows, dig in her heels and brace for impact. Because if the little ship could do something better than any other spacecraft throughout Cassiopeia System, it was landing on a token. And land it did. Hard.

"Cassiopeia Station, this is the *Lazarus*," she sub-voiced in the comms unit strapped to her throat. Unlike other pilots, she hadn't installed any hands-free receivers—plus, she didn't have the kind of money to retrofit the ship's entire electrical grid—and still relied on actual microphones and ear buds to communicate. Obsolete technology for an old-fashioned gal. But still worked like a charm. "I'm powering down."

In the viewscreen above her, a scowling man's face appeared in shades of green and blue. Static from the asteroid belt she'd just cleared still messed transmissions, the main reason communication in these parts had to be done "in person" via uploads and not remote over the links. "Can't you wait for clearance like the rest of the couriers out there?"

She offered him her notorious lopsided grin, which she'd perfected over the years. Part of the carapace she'd built around herself to project only Jackie Clark, the cool, tough courier pilot, while she kept the mellow and jovial Jacqueline private. "The rest of the couriers aren't up to my standards, now are they, Tower?"

Her demanding standards were what kept her above the competition. They also made it possible for her to fulfill the many professional, financial and familial obligations with which she constantly juggled.

He shook his head but smiled. A grumpy old bear. "Yeah, yeah, that's what you young pups all say. Meanwhile, it's Tower who makes sure you don't crash into each other."

She winked at him. "And that's why we all love you so damn much."

"I bet you say that to all the Towers out there."

"What Towers out there?" she replied, cocking her head. "Are there any others out there? You know you're the only one in my heart."

"Just transmit the damn data, would you, and stop tormenting an old man."

She grinned, kissed the air. "Standby for data upload."

The station controller rolled his eyes then reached for something below the viewscreen on his end. "Upload links open. Transmit when ready."

"I love you."

Tower's belly laugh was the last thing she heard as Jackie flicked the comms off then uploaded the data for which she'd risked life and limb. Again. She'd run the lucrative route for years, couriering data to and from Cassiopeia Station—through the deadly asteroid belt—and its various outposts, kept the channels open, the info flowing, because in the dead of space, intel was everything. It meant life or death on certain faraway outposts. She should know. Her parents, who used to run a shuttle service, had become trapped on an outpost when a killer flu outbreak had decimated its population, forcing authorities to seal the airspace. None of the relief runs had arrived on time. They'd both become sick, had never really recovered, lost the business, everything. She'd had to quit her job to be near them. Now six years after and with both of them in a comfortable sanitarium, she was still paying the medical bills. The least she could do.

She hadn't picked up the shuttle business. No money in it. And with both parents under her care, she needed every single credit. Since remote communication was quasi impossible in these parts because of interference, business was booming. Jackie, with her fleet of one ship, the lightweight class *Lazarus*—moniker given by the station's mechanics for her ship's propensity to rise from the dead—had made it her job to deliver the data on time, every time. No cosmic storm or solar flares would keep her on the ground. She'd flown when no one else had, taken assignments no one else could and made a name for herself as one of the few couriers who got the job done. Not bad for a thirty-four-year-old who'd started her company with nothing more than willpower and little collateral for a loan. No one could match her now. Well, except for one other courier.

Jackie closed her eyes for the sheer pleasure of visualizing him. Had she not been up to her eyeballs in bills and responsibility, she would've enjoyed taking a sip of *that* drink.

Terrence "Ty" Weller.

Former colleagues, they'd both started out working for one of the large station conglomerates, spent years brushing elbows and sitting in each other's still-warm seats when switching runs. But if he'd always made her engines rev in every sense of the word, she'd never acted on it. No time for relationships, no energy for anything else but her job and her parents. She didn't want to add another pin to her juggling act. Plus, he wasn't her type. She liked her boyfriends a bit more docile, safer. Ty was anything *but*. She'd never forgotten him though. No way, no sir. It was that voice...

When the data upload terminated, she switched main power off, stretched her tired frame—that'd been one bumpy ride, even by her standards—then stood to get circulation back in her swollen feet. No time to get DVT syndrome. She made a point to exercise as often as she could between runs, not only because gravity was starting to clutch at her butt a bit too firmly, but also to maintain the outward manifestation of the take-no-bull woman. She couldn't very well let her competitors see the softer side of her personality lest they take advantage. Couriering was a dog-eat-dog business. She couldn't afford to lose her reputation, which generated a good portion of the contracts.

As if *Lazarus* meant to remind her he needed parts and a little TLC, steam hissed out of a recently repaired pipe right above her head. Duct tape peeled from the exposed crack.

"I know, babe, I know," she murmured with a pat to the pipe, making a mental note to get to it as soon as the credits were transferred in, which shouldn't take too long with her current client, who always paid well and on time. She'd also need to send some forms back to the sanitarium for added features to her folks' place—another two hundred credits a month right there—then close the books for the fiscal year, revise her budget, remind the dock authorities to update their database—because they *still* had *Lazarus* as medium-class—grab some real food. Maybe try to squeeze a date in edgewise. Ha.

She hadn't taken another step when the comms bleeped at her. The gym would have to wait.

Adrenaline spiked as she rushed back to her seat and turned main power then the viewscreen back on. A face she knew well appeared, distorted by static, straightened. Her best client, architect to the rich and demented—Raymond H. Hillier. He was smiling. Good.

"Jack," he said, his accent still a mystery to her. Something like French but less clipped. Belgian? What did Belgians speak anyway? When he said it, her name sounded like *Jawk*. "Did you just arrive?"

"I did. To what do I owe the pleasure of your fine self in my viewscreen?"

Ray laughed. "Always so smooth. I have a run that requires your expert handling. And this one will pay about two point six, if you are interested."

Her heart thudded once hard then resumed its normal cadence. At two point six mil credits, she'd deliver sewer sludge with her bare hands. "I am very much interested. Can you give me some details?"

"It is a tight deadline," he began, taking his time, smoothing his salt-and-pepper mustache. "And you will run with another courier as backup—"

Backup equals delays, equals loss of profit and control, equals big heap of trouble...

"Excuse me," she cut in through a tight smile. "I don't really need a backup."

He shook his head. "No, but *I* do. You run the first upload then Terrence will run the backup in case of... Well, you know, fiery death and all that."

"Terrence Weller is my backup?"

"Have you worked with him in the past?" He smiled, a smug, mustachioed cat sitting on the fence.

"Yes."

She had more to say but her pride had to take a backseat to her business sense, which, luckily for her, tended to kick in whenever an outrageous amount of credits was mentioned. She *needed* those credits.

Ray picked lint from his black shirt lapel. "This run requires the finest couriers in the system. You both are it."

She offered him her infamous grin. Wondered if he could tell she'd rather chew bees. "I would work better alone, Ray."

"I disagree. Quicker perhaps, but not better."

Jackie fought against the impulse to slam her foot in the screen and instead clamped her mouth shut for fear she'd say something that would lose her the contract. *The client is always right. The client is always right. The client...*

17

Deep breath.

She'd always had a temper. Her mom's side, or so her dad maintained. Then again, each parent claimed she'd inherited her big mouth from the other. But over the years of running her own courier service, she'd learned a thing or two about human nature and business. First, everyone had their own agenda and deadlines and tried their best. Second, no one wanted to deal with attitude. And third, with a bit of age had come the sagacity to realize she'd attract more flies with honey than vinegar. Plus, sometimes a woman had to learn to just *breathe*.

"At two point six, I figured it would compensate for the aggravation of working with another courier. Perhaps I should secure a differ—"

"Just a moment, if you would," she interrupted before he could cut her off at the knees and offer the astronomical sum to a competitor. "I'm feeling a bit of a catch here, Ray. If it's anything illegal, you know I won't touch it. A woman has her standards."

His eyes narrowed while he grinned. Oh, he had her and the arrogant jerk knew it.

"It could not be more legal, I assure you. You've heard of that new station going up off the nebula? I'm bidding for the spaceport's contracts. So I need plans from my chief designer and he is on Titan Five right now. It's the deadline that is driving up the price. It is tight, as I mentioned. Twenty-four hours to get the data from Titan Five then back here."

"Twenty-four hours," she repeated calmly, smile still in place, even if on the inside she was yanking her hair out by the fistful. That was an *insane* deadline, even for her. Barely time to reach the destination, refuel and race back.

"Two point six mil, Jack. If you need time to think about it…"

"You *know* I'm the only one who can handle that kind of run. I'm on."

"You *and* Terrence."

Had this meeting been conducted in person, she would've needed several deep breaths not to punch his lights out. With a forced, "My pleasure, goodbye, Ray," she cut the comms link then stomped across the plated deck.

A backup. Ugh. She'd have to fly with someone else, adjust her ways, change what worked to suit another's style and agenda. Relinquish a bit of control to another. No time for that.

Jackie pinched the bridge of her nose against the mounting pressure as she paced back and forth. There never was any *time*. She needed a clone.

"Breathe," she said out loud.

Unless he'd changed and gone soft, Ty was more than capable, but he'd better make sure because she couldn't afford to take him by the hand. Twenty-four hours to fly through the dreaded asteroid belt twice, or the "Valley of Death" as someone had aptly dubbed it, download the data from the source on Titan Five Colony then rush back to Cassiopeia Station to upload it to Ray's account. Demented.

"But two point six mil."

She whooped, punched the air in a one-two combination. That'd take care of the hospice's bill for the rest of the year, maybe leave a little extra for some parts for her ship. And so opportune.

Fifteen minutes later, showered, fueled up on caffeine and only slightly less agitated, Jackie was pacing the cramped flight deck of her cruiser when the comms console bleeped. Punctual. They'd never really done runs together, had only worked around the other for a couple years before she'd had to fly to her parents' bedside. But from what she remembered, Ty's punctuality was only second to his bad temper. There'd been couriers who'd refused to fly with him. She could understand. The guy was scary. Sexy as all hell, but *dangerous*.

She pressed on the Receive button, eyes on the screen and fighting down the eagerness of seeing his face again. In disappointing audio only, her viewscreen showed a place-holder logo depicting an eagle in flight, its taloned feet clutched over a scroll. She'd much rather have visuals too, just to get a look at him. Had he changed over the years? Was he as handsome as before or had time been unkind to the man who'd so thoroughly made her hot around the collar?

"Clark here," she said as she strapped the sub-voicer to her throat. "How have you been?"

"I couldn't have been better without breaking some law," came the throaty voice she remembered so well. Like a harsh whisper in the throes of passion. Shivers made her roll her shoulders. He sounded just the way she remembered. "You? Life treating you well?" he asked.

"Up until now, yes," she said through a grin.

"As charming as I remember."

"Well, I'm glad I made a lasting impression on you." And she had the whole-body frisson to prove it. He chuckled. Things weren't turning out to be so bad after—

"You sure did, gorgeous," he went on.

Gorgeous...?

"Did you just call me 'gorgeous'?"

"Nope."

"Yes, you did. You said 'you sure did, gorgeous'. That's what you said, *Terrence*."

Another chuckle. "What, gorgeous? You gonna sue me for emotional distress? And the name's Ty, you know that."

"Ha! I only wish I had time to sue." She dropped her voice a notch. "But I *am* going to make you eat my space dust, Mister."

"Mmm. I'd eat anything of yours you want me to."

She hadn't remembered *that* part. When had he become flirty? Maybe the big scary guy had mellowed over the years?

The loaded remark created pleasant tingles all along her spine. That voice hadn't changed one bit, just as sexy and seductive as she remembered. To this day, nothing had ever compared to the physical reaction that voice could trigger.

"Did you get the brief?" she asked, pinching the flight suit's collar to vent out some of the heat. "Are you ready to roll?"

"I did and I am. I'm about to rendezvous with your ship's coordinates. Should be able to see me on your viewscreen right now. *If* your ship has 'em. From what I can see, it belongs in a museum. You sure you'll be able to keep up in that old thing?"

"Old thing, huh?" she muttered as she spared a glance at her nav console, spotted the tiny yellow dot with its tag and nomenclature shooting toward her position just out of the station's airspace. The guy's ship was *fast*. Damn him.

"I have you on my radar."

"Good, I like being on a gal's radar," he replied, and even if she couldn't see his face, she knew he was smiling. Having fun at her expense. "Makes me all kinds of tingly."

"I'm powering up now. Try not to get lost, *Terrence*."

"Same to you, *gorgeous*."

Just to show him she could pull her own, and *Lazarus* still had it in him despite the repairs, the duct tape and the years, Jackie fired the boosters in a brusque flare that made her old ship groan and creak in protest. Pitch up, left wing down, she tore out of Cassiopeia airspace as if her tail were on fire. Had to keep the reputation intact. Couldn't back down and roll over. Appearances were everything in her business. As much as she enjoyed the man's voice and hot body, Ty still remained a competitor.

"Damn! Thanks a lot," she heard Ty grumble over the comms. "You just wiped out half my starboard fore sensors."

Jackie quickly stamped down the spike of guilt. "Sorry, Ty. I'll slow down for you, okay?"

All she heard was a muttered comment that contained several variants of the f-word. She hadn't technically meant to fry his sensors, only show him she could pull her own weight, that her reputation wasn't fluff but deserved and earned. That standing put food on her table.

Maybe she'd buy him a beer or something, make it up to him after the run. Possibly negotiate him a couple of sensors from her suppliers, who could get them cheap and fast. With two point six mil credits in her pocket, she'd be able to afford a few extra sensors.

Jackie leaned back as Gs accumulated and pressed her into the synthetic leather seat, which creaked and rattled on its steel pedestal moorings. Somewhere below deck, a *thunk* reverberated. Her ship would need some extra love after this run. She hadn't even had time to fix the burst pipe whistling not far behind her. Next break. Two point six million credits wouldn't come her way anytime soon. And even if she had to put up with another courier as backup—the infamous Terrence Weller on top of things—the money more than made up for the irritation. And the danger. Crossing the asteroid belt twice in twenty-four hours, after an earlier run, was like poking good fortune in the eye with a sharp stick. Both eyes even.

She had to grudgingly admit to herself Ty was one fine pilot. Always had been. He maneuvered his much larger and newer, fancier, shinier—damn him—ship in smooth rolls and precise banks, sometimes coming so close to her hull her prox alerts would bleep. He did it on purpose too, of that she had no doubt. Although to be fair, she *had* acted like an ass for powering up so fast and so close to another ship.

"So," Ty crooned directly into her skull because of the ear bud. "You left in a hurry. Last I heard, you were on a run for New Bombay. And unlike the cat, you never came back."

Despite the separation years and a hectic lifestyle provided, she could still see it in her mind as vividly as if it'd happened that morning. She'd been halfway to her destination when she received the urgent news about her parents' situation, the desperate call for couriers to bring in aid, the government dragging its feet, claiming red tape and whatnot. She'd quit the same day, transferred the cargo to another courier then spent months at the hospital feeding jelly to her mom and dad. And the smell. Their poor, ruined bodies. Her mom who'd been pleasantly plump before her illness, and her dad with his mischievous grin, which she hadn't seen since. They did better now, of course, but the memory of their frailty still followed her around like a disproportionate shadow. Every call could be The Call.

Jackie shook her head as if she could dislodge the old fears. "Life happens. You know how it goes."

"Yeah. What've you been up to all that time? Married? Kids?"

"No. You?"

A quick bark of laughter. "You think a gal would put up with my shit?"

"Not really."

"You didn't have to agree."

"But I'm so agreeable."

"Now that, I honestly don't remember about you," Ty replied, teasing.

Jackie laughed, couldn't help it. Neither could she help the fire from spreading over her back, up her neck and to her cheeks. His voice had always had that effect on her. "Let's hear what else you remember then."

"Let me see," he began slowly. She heard a wet sound over the comms and guessed he was doing something with his mouth, which produced another wave of liquid fire and a fine spike of sexual energy. "Bad temper, big mouth, hot body. And a cute little dimple when you go sulking off."

"I do not sulk."

"You do, gorgeous." He must have done that thing with his mouth again. The wet sound revved her engines as bad as his voice. "Sexy."

She didn't sulk, did she? That would neutralize all the hard work she put in her reputation, let people see the tender inside. Not acceptable in her line of business. That she had a temper was no news flash, but that she was inherently a gentle soul could hinder her. As a chief competitor, he might get ideas, take advantage.

But she did *not* sulk. Of this she was sure.

"You're tailing, gorgeous," Ty remarked. She realized she *had* slowed as she overanalyzed his remark and did tail his ship by a couple of miles. "You like coming in from behind?" he added.

Men. "Would you just focus and stop thinking about behinds?"

"Oh I am. I'm very, very *focused* right now."

When she didn't reply, he chuckled. Probably proud of himself too. The next twenty-four hours would feel more like years. She reclaimed her spot as first courier with Ty keeping his ship a tight quarter mile behind. Jackie wondered what he thought of playing backup. Not letting the order of their ships—and Ray's calling sequence—get to her head was, well, kind of hard. He'd called *her* for first position. She was the main courier, not the backup. The years of hard work and sacrifice were paying off. Financially anyway.

After a couple of light-years, they approached the asteroid belt. Most couriers and civilian ships traveled *around* the dangerous zone, which meant twice the time and twice the fuel, and not right *through* it. But in her business, time was money. She couldn't afford delays. Plus, sometimes the data needed to get there fast—like medical or diplomatic stuff—and couldn't be distributed through the regular, governmental channels. Too slow. She should know. Hence the need for folks like her. Pilots reckless enough—or dumb enough, depending on the point of view—to courier the goods.

On her screen, the asteroids resembled a ribbon of tiny chunks of ice and rocks circling a giant gas planet—even if in reality the "tiny" chunks were the size of skyscrapers. She'd always loved that planet, loved its marbled colors—coronas of blues and greens and purples—with its roiling surface of hydrogen and helium. Like a giant Saturn.

The belt's twinkling made Jackie's eyes water so she glanced at the other ship and grinned when, given the iridescent light, she found it resembled a long silver penis with stunted wings and a trio of supercharged boosters at the base. The imagery made her chuckle. Pretty much summed up Terrence Weller. A big dick. Ha.

But that voice...

Jackie pulled at her collar to let some of the heat out of her one-piece flight suit. A guy with a voice like that could whisper all kinds of things in her ear. She wouldn't mind!

"Are you ready, gorgeous?" His gravelly voice filled her brain, tightened her nape and caused serious heat to flare out of her suit.

All she could manage was one word. "Yes."

"Mmm, like the sound of that."

"I thought you preferred the sound of your own voice."

He laughed. "Got some tongue on you, Clark. I like that."

"So do I."

"An invitation?"

"Not really."

"That's too bad then," he said. "See you on the other side."

"If you get pulverized, can I have your ship for parts?"

"And if *you* get mashed up, can I get your—oh wait, your ship's crap. Never mind. Switching to short range."

25

After she likewise switched the comms relay to short-range so the belt wouldn't cause interference, Jackie muttered a curse. "Har-har."

Chewing her lip, Jackie killed the main engine and prepared to enter the "Valley of Death". Nothing like a good, scary moniker to secure people's undivided attention. It sure had hers. She'd learned early in her career to respect big, giant rocks floating in space.

For the first couple of hours all went well. She'd use the gravitational pull to dodge smaller asteroids, fly around those too large or too quick for her to match with brusque, economical half bursts. Behind and a quarter mile to portside, Ty preferred to give full bursts of attitude jets instead. Must have plenty of fuel in that fancy ship. Yeah, well, *Lazarus* would still make him eat space dust.

"So far so good," he said. His voice sounded tight. She wondered if he stuck his tongue out when he concentrated. The incongruous thought made her snort a quick laugh. She shouldn't think about his mouth. If she remembered correctly—and dammit, she did—it was luscious...except when he was pissed, then it'd thin to a menacing line.

"Something I said?"

"Would you just leave me alone for a second?" She fired a quick burst of attitude jets. Perfect timing.

"Ouch. I'm not used to women telling me to leave them alone."

"Oh and humble too."

"As humble as you're charming, gorgeous."

One of her prox alerts bleeped so she changed headings, prepared to swerve over the large spinning asteroid coming at her when in one of her viewscreens, she spotted another smaller rock twirling behind its large companion, effectively hiding in its shadow. Tricky little thing. The size of a shuttle but still large enough to make a nice dent in *Lazarus*. But she'd seen it and would adjust course accordingly.

"Front and center," she remarked, all business. "Be careful."

"Got it."

Behind her, Ty didn't adjust course. For some reason, he'd decided to play chicken with ten tons of silicate, iron and nickel traveling at fifteen point five miles a second. What was up with him?

"I said front and center," she repeated, leaning forward to tap her O2 gauges. Had to have the right mix or *Lazarus* would go *boom* and wouldn't rise from the dead again.

"I said I got it, gorgeous."

At one thousand feet away, she lifted her wing, let the smaller asteroid pass under then leveled off a split second before all kinds of bells and whistles filled her deck.

Damn!

Both hands went flying over controls at once. But no lights flashed other than the prox alerts, which would blink until she'd cleared the veritable space minefield. It took her a second to realize the cacophony of warnings came through the comms. From Ty's ship not hers.

"What's going on?" she sub-voiced, leaning forward to take a look at the rear viewscreen. "Pitch up!"

"Motherf—"

Static drowned the rest of his snarled reply. Even though it hadn't happened on her ship, she still felt a weird shock traverse her and a sense of alarm she'd never experienced before.

Oh. Shit.

The smaller asteroid had just collided with Ty's ship. A glancing hit on starboard, right where he'd said her little stunt had fried some of his exterior sensors.

"Are you all right?" she yelled to be heard above the shrill sirens of his ship. Judging by the sound, hull integrity had been breached. Double shit.

"I'm losing O2!" he roared. "Breach imminent!"

Guilt flooded her judgment for a good second. She'd crippled him right out the gate. It was her fault he hadn't seen the smaller asteroid coming. She didn't mind giving him hell and all that, especially for old times' sake, but she hadn't meant to destroy his ship and kill him.

"Suit up! I'll get you!"

"Are you nuts?" he snarled, still obviously fighting with his controls when he should've been trying to get the hell out of his doomed ship.

"Suit *up!*"

"There's no *time* to put on a motherfucking suit!"

Damn.

He couldn't escape his ship without a suit, didn't have time to put one on in the first place. They needed a way for him to get out...

An idea struck her. A crazy, dementedly dangerous idea. They'd only have one shot at it, and if he didn't take it now, he'd end up an icicle stuck to his seat. She wasn't prepared to live with that kind of weight on her conscience. She might be considered a ruthless courier, all business and nothing else, but that wasn't her inside, that wasn't Jacqueline. And she sure wasn't a killer!

"Pitch up!" she yelled in the mike strapped to her throat. "Roll forty-five degrees to starboard side!"

Even if he must have been wondering what she meant to do, he rolled to the right and lifted his left wing at forty-five degrees, effectively presented his ship's belly to hers. The coupling hatch gleamed like black ink on the silver underbelly.

"Unlock your hatch!"

"What the fuck are you doing?"

Jackie cursed. "Unlock your goddamn hatch, Weller! Now!"

He must have understood her plan—and appropriately thought she'd had something stronger than milk in her cereal that morning—but the man still maintained his course, belly-up her side while she mirrored the position. With good fortune willing, their bellies and hatches would meet in the middle. He'd have ten seconds tops to unlock his hatch, transfer ships then crawl out of her airlock and onto the main deck. If he failed at any of it, his ship would detach, spilling its content—Terrence Weller included—into space for her to watch. Not acceptable.

"Keep it steady," she said for no good reason other than the need to let some steam out. "Keep it steady…"

"I *am!*" he growled, cursed when another alarm added its high-pitched self to the mix. "Fuck! Losing fuel now too!"

But he clung to his heading and attitude, kept his hull presented to her as two birds would flying side by side with their bellies about to touch in the middle.

Twenty feet.

God, she'd never flown this close to another ship before. One tiny miscalculation or twitch of the hand and Ray would have to find someone else to get his precious plans.

Ten feet.

Such a tiny target.

Five.

Prox alerts blared by the time his ship's belly connected against hers. A deep *thunk* reverberated when the mooring clamps snapped into place. She felt *Lazarus* slow down with the added mass and drag.

"Do it! Now!" she yelled under the strain of keeping both ships in position.

Three hundred miles ahead and coming at them at an angle, an asteroid the size of a small planet lazily twirled. If it hit, they wouldn't suffer long. Like bugs on a windshield.

She heard him curse then nothing but sirens and alarms wailing. For a few seconds, Jackie wondered if he'd made it. Where the hell was he? She had to jettison the dead weight of his ship or risk joining it when the asteroid hit. On the dirty chronoclock taped to the nav console, ten seconds became nine, eight, seven.

"Come *on*," she snarled, bent over the controls, ready to retract the hatch and blow the other ship off.

Her ship's airlock light blinked on at the edge of the screen, warning her someone had activated it from the outside. Good man.

Six, five, four...

"Shit... Come on, come on, come *on!*"

Jackie put her thumb against the button that would start the jettison sequence, hoping he'd made it. The airlock light blinked off. If he'd failed and gone back to his ship, or hadn't had time to crawl into the pressurized portion of hers, then there was nothing she could do. She should've already changed course to avoid the now-looming asteroid.

Three, two, one.

"Sorry, Ty, I just can't wait anymore."

Jackie thumbed the control. With a pair of *clangs*, the mooring clamps opened, releasing Ty's ship, and with a loud *pof*, her hatch retracted into her vessel's belly, which sent the other craft rolling away, its own hatch gaping wide.

"Shit, shit, shit," she hissed as she re-pressurized her airlock. What if he hadn't made it? What had she done! With trembling fingers, she pressed the internal comms. "Ty? Are you there? *Ty?*"

Ominous silence answered her.

Sweat dripped from her temple down along her jaw as she fought against the urge to check below deck and ascertain his physical state. He'd be pissed off, of that she had no doubt. His temper sure hadn't mellowed *that* much, despite the new flirty side. But what if he was badly hurt? Dying in her airlock?

She tried the internal comms again. "Ty? Damn, Ty, respond!"

What if he hadn't made it? Maybe he was floating in space, cursing her with his last breath.

A sound behind her caught her attention. She spun the seat on its pedestal so she could partly face the hatch and still keep an eye on the consoles. Her breath caught.

A man was stepping through the hatch.

He wore a synthetic and oh-so-shiny black T-shirt stretched over a partitioned chest and belly of perfect proportions and symmetry, and olive-green cargo pants that highlighted one fine pair of muscled thighs. He stomped onto her flight deck in black military-issue boots. She'd forgotten just how *big* he was in person. If she'd thought he'd mellowed with the years...how wrong she'd been. Terrence Weller had become even bigger, dangerous-looking and scarier. Still the same six feet of shaven-smooth head and face, wicked-sexy mouth stretched over a rictus of rage that would've made her mother sign herself. Twice. He'd added an eyebrow ring to his looks, but the rest was unchanged. The same wolfish expression on his hard face and lean lines, the same fire glowing like coals behind his dark eyes. He'd always reminded her of an actor back in old 2-D movies, a Vincent, Vince something with a last name like "fuel". Very large, very scary. It was hard to think beyond that point.

And he didn't look happy one bit.

Chapter Two

ဆ

So there she was back in his life again. Jackie Clark.

Damn, how long had it been? Six years and some change? For the two they'd worked together at a now-defunct courier conglomerate, he'd walked around in a constant state of horniness—and crankiness—because the ambitious, driven, take-no-bullshit little firebrand had embodied everything he enjoyed in women. A tough exterior and, he suspected, a soft inside. Loved that mix. But before he'd cleaned up, worked out a few details in his life—details like clawing his way out of some bad company and worse connections, maybe even a bit of organized crime somewhere in the mix—she'd pulled a disappearing act on him. One day she was there and the next she was gone. He'd learned afterward his favorite pilot had started her own biz. Figured she didn't need ghosts of the past to tag along and had left it at that. But shit, Jackie had stirred his blood in a serious way.

His blind spot.

And now she'd just cost him his ship. The one thing he owned fair and square, the one damn thing his failed manufacturer of an old man hadn't been able to drink or gamble away, the means to pay for his baby sister's education. If one miserable Weller could claw up to being a doctor, an honest and meaningful job for a change, he sure as hell was going to help. Lydia *would* graduate top of her class if he had to beat the shit out of the dean, *would* go on and make her professional worrier of a big brother proud and maybe even put a bit of shine back on the Weller family crest. Because as it stood now, they had a crooked industrialist, a former drug runner and a nonexistent mother who'd run off with a guy half her age after the birth of her "surprise" child Lydia. At sixteen,

Ty had basically raised her. Not that he blamed his mom for dumping his old man. But leaving the kids behind?

His ship had been *every-fucking-thing*. And now it was gone. Murder on his mind and in his hands, Ty cleared the low-hanging hatch. His rage filled the flight deck almost like a physical thing.

He had plenty of reasons to kick her ass from here to Cassiopeia Station and back again. A good round of size-twelve boots would do her good, the mouthy little shit. Mouthy, spicy little hottie. *That* he remembered perfectly well. How could he have forgotten when the gal had become the barometer by which he'd measured all other women? Right now though, he didn't care if she'd become even sexier with some years to her.

Yeah right.

Damn hormones. During the two seconds it took him to clear the hatch and come face-to-face with the reason he was now a penniless nobody with not a single goddamn rivet to his name, his rage mutated into something completely different. He went from wanting to kill her with his bare hands to fighting the hard-on triggered by the vision in front of him. That she still sat in her seat, clearly unimpressed, only poured jet fuel by the gallons on the inferno burning his balls. Christ, just his luck. He should've expected it. Nothing was simple with Jackie Clark around. And he was now stuck with her on a tiny, tiny ship. Fuck.

"You," he snarled, leveling an accusing index finger at her. He was so goddamn pissed, he was shaking all over. "You... You..." He'd never called a woman the names that piled into his mouth and wasn't about to start now, but dammit if he wasn't burning to. "Your little stunt..." He puffed a few times to let some of the steam out. "It just cost me my goddamn ship."

She sat there still, the determined expression he remembered, five and a half feet of—short, nowadays—hair, almond-shaped dark eyes, pinched mouth and attitude. He'd called her his Asian Goddess of Fury. No change there. She wasn't a bombshell by any stretch of the imagination. Never had been. Jaw too square, smallish breasts, unstyled hair still damp from a recent shower and starting to stick up in places — the whole fucking flight deck smelled of soap and wasn't helping his focus. Nothing beat eating pussy that smelled of soap. Mmm. But what she lacked in fashionable beauty, she'd always more than made up for in intensity and physical strength. In the tight flight suit the color of a dirty sky, she had shoulders that'd put swimmers to shame. So she'd gone to the gym too, added some inches to her, gained a bit of welcomed weight. He loved good strong shoulders in a woman, made perfect anchors when they sucked his dick. The vision of Jackie on her knees, fucking his cock with her mouth, burned the last of his failing neurons. Plus, she had freckles. He had *loved* those from the start. What sort of man didn't want to fuck a gal with freckles!

He shook his head to scramble the stupid images. Shit on a stick! "You fucked everything up, Clark."

"No, I didn't," she replied, clearly awed after she threw a quick glance at the console. "Look at *that*."

The screen that showed the planet's curvature and part of the asteroid belt must've been older than both of them combined. To his shock, he spotted his ship twirl clear of the asteroids through some cosmic twist he couldn't explain and float belly-up just outside the danger zone. By a cunt hair, but still in the clear. Too bad couriers couldn't fly in lower orbit since it wasted too much fuel fighting against the gravitational pull. Instead they had to fly through the belt, figuratively running across a twenty-lane boulevard and hoping no car would hit them. Although his ship had just managed it without pilot or propulsion.

To his utter amazement, within seconds his ship had entered the gas giant's lower orbit right below the asteroid belt where it'd remain until salvagers came to tow it after the thirty-day wait. Without a ride, he wouldn't be able to claim his ship back.

"Well, fuck me."

She cleared her throat. "You can find a ride to get it back. I'll get you one."

He gave her his best glare. "If you feel as stupid and guilty as you look, then that's a good first step, Clark, because you ought to."

"Look—"

"No, you 'look'! You think I have a spare ship waiting at home, all nice and shiny?"

His tone must have raised her hackles because she stuck her chin out at him. Old times. He'd enjoyed watching her take a few strips off people when they'd crossed her. "Hey, it was an accident, okay?"

"An accident my ass. You powered up not even a hundred feet in front of my nose. You did it on purpose." He wondered for a crazy second that had nothing to do with the present situation, if she enjoyed being on top. He loved watching his lovers bounce on him. The larger the breasts the better. He had big hands, he could manage.

Black eyes narrowed to slits. Her cheeks were flushed while that dimple he'd loved deepened. Sexy.

"I didn't mean to wreck your sensors, Ty!"

"Yeah, well, you did. So now what?"

"I don't know," she sighed, threw her hands up.

He cut a glance at the screen again, followed his ship's leisurely journey. He'd just hightailed it out of his ship for nothing? Maybe he could've saved it, stayed a few seconds more and try to fix the breach. The more he thought about it, the more he knew fixing his ship in time wouldn't have happened. He would've died of asphyxiation or explosive depressurization, sucked out into space with the rest of the loose bits floating around his ship. Or crashed head-on into the asteroid he hadn't spotted in time since she'd goddamn fried half his sensors right out the gate.

Cocky little bitch. He should kick her ass. Yeah. Give it a good bite too just for the fuck of it. Maybe a lick.

But.

There was always a but.

Even if she'd created the problem to begin with, Jackie Clark had still come and helped when it would've been easy to just sit back and watch the lightshow. Hell, that's what *he* would've done in her boots. Sit back, get some popcorn and a cold beer, watch the competition go out in a hail of titanium rivets. That was the Jackie Clark he remembered. Nothing came for free with her. But she'd just put her own ship and life in danger when she realized he hadn't seen the asteroid as it twirled at him and stayed put for the most dangerous and harebrained space transfer he'd ever heard of. Switching ships in the fucking Valley of Death. Well, shit, if that didn't turn a man on, he didn't know what would. His cock thought so too and hardened at the idea. Still, he owed her one and was about to deliver it.

Ty stalked to her seat, leaned on both armrests and put his face right up to hers. If she was impressed, she didn't let it show. The smell of soap dispersed his chain of thought for a good five seconds. Christ. "I have half a mind to kick your ass for what you did."

"You try, big guy," she snarled, lowering her chin.

The way she put a nonchalant hand over the harness buckle told him he'd get one good shot before she kicked his balls. But that'd be all he'd need, really, one shot.

So that standoff, it's going where again, hero?

"You think I wouldn't 'cause you're a woman?" He hoped he didn't look as off course as he felt. He *wouldn't* hit a woman of course, but he couldn't very well let her think she had the last word. Hell no!

She narrowed her eyes, cocked her head. "Oh, I'm sure you can beat on a woman with no problem. You always looked the part to me. Even more so now with that fancy ring."

Hey.

A prox alert saved him from replying to the cheap shot. He wasn't a woman beater. He may only be a couple of notches up from thug—his old man liked reminding him of that among other things—but he wasn't a brute.

"Your ship's talking to you," he snarled, hooking a thumb at the flashing console. Saved face at least. He straightened, crossed his arms.

She peered over her shoulder, cursed. "Hang on!"

Before he could—and to what should he "hang on" anyway, the flight deck was the size of his closet and just as dumpy—she'd whirled her seat around, furiously clicked on the console with one hand while she gripped the control stick with the other. Not imagining it was his dick was pretty damn hard. His old crush was coming back full force and he suspected there wouldn't be a damn thing he could do about it.

He felt Gs accumulating then grunted when she rolled to the left, ignored the cacophony of signals and alarms her stunt had caused, ignored *him* as well when he went flying across the deck to bang against upright consoles and become tangled in wires.

"For fuck's sake, Jackie!"

But she had her hands full. On the screen, a cluster of asteroids was coming at them hard and fast. Instead of veering away and flying up around them, as any pilot with half a brain would've, the crazy woman leveled off, aimed dead center.

"What the—?!"

He barely had time to curse when she flew her old clunker between the three middle asteroids, right wing straight up. At the last possible second she rolled to avoid the rest of the chunks hurtling at them left, right and sideways.

Shit. Shit. He'd postponed dying on his own ship only to be blasted into bits on someone else's? Crazy woman. But he had to admit her fine handling had just procured him with one thrilling jab of sexual energy to zing up his thighs and tighten his dick even more. He loved women with balls. Well, not *literally*.

She turned back, noticed he wasn't where he'd been before her stunt then offered him a lopsided grin that just about made him want to pounce on her and chew her clothes off. He was *so* getting inside that flight suit. The sooner the better too.

"Are you okay, Ty? You look pale."

"When we're in the clear, I'm gonna show you just how 'okay' I am."

A slow grin rounded her cheek. "Is that right?"

"Hell yeah!"

She still smiled. This time, a wicked lift to her lips and a glint of something raw in her gaze made him salivate. She was just as turned-on as he was. Well, the little vixen.

Maybe he should've pursued the matter back when they worked together and gotten her out of his system, scratched the itch once and for all since it didn't seem to be going anywhere. He had his chance now.

Ty turned out to be the worst kind of backseat pilot she'd ever seen. Each maneuver she executed was dissected, commented on, picked apart, cursed at. Instead of just sitting tight—on the deck too, poor guy—and shutting his big trap, Ty acted as if he had to provide a running commentary of her flying and complained the whole way through the asteroid belt, even remarking how lucky they were to be alive given her ship's age. It had nothing to do with luck, dammit. She should've spaced his cute butt instead of taking him onboard. Finally, they cleared the danger zone, which allowed her a good roll of the shoulders to alleviate the tension. Mostly caused by her "passenger".

Standing, she turned to him just as he peeled himself off the deck, massaging his shoulder and grumbling curses about the lack of "proper seats on this goddamn old clunker". Always complaining. She took the comms unit from her breast pocket, pulled out the ear bud and unclipped the mike from her throat then tossed everything on the seat. A couple of hours on autopilot to wind down before they reached Titan Five, collected the data then rushed back to upload everything to Ray's account. She needed even more coffee and lots of it.

"Do you ever stop talking to breathe?" she snapped.

"Learn to pilot and I might," he shot back, blocking the hatch when she aimed for it.

"I'm an *excellent* pilot."

"In your dreams, maybe. You almost killed us half a dozen times, for fuck's sake. I don't remember you being so damn reckless."

"Those were calculated risks. And this is the gratitude I get for saving you?"

"*Saving* me? After you all but blinded me?" he snarled, his anger filling the tiny flight deck.

Something else also filled her space—lust. Even after six years, she still thought he was the sexiest guy this side of the Falcon Nebula. Tanned and muscled, stubborn and loud. The shaven head, wicked mouth and new eyebrow ring didn't help either.

"You know what they say, if you can't take the heat..."

His dark eyes narrowed dangerously and she knew she'd pushed a button a bit too deep. Ty took a step. Just one. But it almost made her take one back. Almost. Only pride riveted her to the spot despite every instinct clamoring for her to put as much distance as possible between the large angry man and her.

"I've got plenty of heat, don't worry about me. But that's my ship out there that I paid with my own cash, floating belly-up like a dead fish. And you're gonna pay for the repairs or find me a salvage crew to get it back."

"As if I have that kind of credit in my pockets?"

"Not now," he replied with a triumphant sort of smile that didn't sit well with her. "But soon you will. You're about to get two point six mil, if I remember correctly, and a whole lot of time off if I report your ass to the guild."

"I'm getting one point four," she replied without meeting his gaze. "And the guild has better things to do than take care of creaky wheels." Inside, she cringed. She didn't need another row with the couriers' guild, who were waiting to find an excuse to yank her permit. Damn.

"You were never a good liar, Jackie. I guess that can be a good thing. Depends who you hang out with."

He took another step. Stood barely a couple of inches from her, clouded her judgment with his male scent and gorgeous mouth and perfect chest underneath the tight black T-shirt. What he could do with that mouth...the stuff of dreams. As she had then, she again wondered what sort of women he preferred, how many girlfriends he'd accumulated, if he was a talker in bed, but also the sort of upbringing that made a man such as Terrence Weller. He wasn't trouble or some cookie-cutter rebel. Neither did he portray a "bad boy" image for the simple reason that Ty was a *man*, not a boy, with no affected bravado. The cloud of menace permanently hanging over his head, it was for real. His unusual sort of beauty transcended every stereotype.

"You're getting the same cut I am," he went on in that hoarse voice, which did nothing to help her focus. "But the deal's changed now. You're gonna give me half so I can get a salvager to tow my ship back. Then you're gonna finance the repairs too."

The pleasant tingle of sexual awareness evaporated like fog in a wind tunnel. Who did he think he was? Her temper had never flared so bad, so quick. She planted her fists on her hips. Heat wafted out of her zipped-down flight suit. "*What?* Finance your repairs?"

"Hell yeah." He cocked his pierced eyebrow, took a good look from her boots to the top of her head. Which was about to blow off with the mad she was working on. The gall!

"Are you out of your *mind?*"

Ty gave her another pronounced once-over, his mouth curving at one corner. Oh hell, that was one sexy smirk. "You don't wanna know what's on my mind, Jackie. Let's just stick to the biz, okay?"

"I have connections, I'll see what I can do, but you're not getting half my cut. As for your mind," she went on, letting her gaze travel down the length of him the way he'd just done with her. "I know exactly where it is."

Where her own had been the entire time. In the gutter.

"You do?" The sexy curve to his mouth accentuated. "It means yours is there too."

"No, it doesn't," she replied a bit too fast. The heat of anger turned into something else. She swallowed.

"You're such a bad liar. Always were."

Jackie crossed her arms just in case she didn't appear composed enough—which was a lie, damn him. She wanted him in a bad way.

Ty looked down at himself, grinned as he patted his crotch. "What can I say, I've always had a weak spot for you."

He had?

"A weak spot?" she retorted. "For me? Since when?"

"Since I saw you demolish that locker door," he said before tucking his bottom lip behind his teeth. It gave him a predatory air. She loved it. "Remember that one? In the cargo bay. You were trying to get into your locker and it wouldn't open?"

"I remember." Her supervisors had deducted her pay for the repairs. She'd been in a hurry. The story of her life.

"Turned me on hard enough to see stars," he said. "Like right now."

Her gaze slid down his chest and belly, both of which looked rock-hard and tantalizing enough to touch, down to his crotch again where a lump strained the cargo pants along the inside of his muscled thigh. Her palms itched to cup all that hot man. His T-shirt looked as if it'd been painted on, shiny black with the synthetic fabric.

"See something you like?" he asked, pierced brow arched. That throaty voice was doing wonders to her imagination again. Having a guy with a voice like that could probably make her sweat just by whispering wicked things in her ear.

She shrugged, all cool composure even if inside she'd become a hormonal mess. "Do *you*?"

"You *know* it."

"Mmm, I don't know," she replied. Rising blood pressure began a rhythmic *whoosh-whoosh* in her ears. "You can never tell with these things."

She stopped breathing when he extended a hand, pinched the lapel of her flight suit in thick, strong fingers then gently pulled sideways to expose a bit of her black tank top. She noticed he chewed his nails bad.

"You gals are lucky. It doesn't show when you're turned-on. Not like us guys."

She hooked her thumb in her pocket just to give herself something to do. Half of her wanted to kick his butt and get him off her ship, but the other half wanted to do very different sorts of things to her passenger, things that years before had made her call a lover "Ty" by mistake.

"Maybe I am, maybe I'm not," she replied, feeling stupid for the way her voice sounded tight and tremulous. "I've changed, Ty. I'm no longer the young woman you worked with."

"You've more than changed," he replied, licking his bottom lip. "You've become even better. And it's turning me on, Jackie. You have no idea."

"Turned-on is a good thing. Natural response. Instincts. Women have all that too."

"I know, gorgeous. I *know.*"

Each nerve ending felt on fire, each sweat pore prickled, each hair on her arms stood at attention. That he had her absolute attention would be the understatement of the century. With the sensualization he'd triggered then and now, with the vivid images of his body moving against hers came a wave of heat, a rush of adrenaline that left her wanting him. Fiercely. An old hunger.

"Let's say you do," he replied, his voice a notch above a murmur. His nostrils flared. "Mmm? Let's say you *do* see something you like. Are you the kinda gal who'll go and take it, or wait 'til it comes to you? Are you still the Jackie Clark I once knew?"

"What do you think?"

Don't look at his mouth, don't look at his mouth. She couldn't focus and play cool cucumber if she looked at his wicked, sexy mouth. Never could.

He crowded her against the bulkhead, his wide chest and shoulders so tempting in the black T-shirt, his chin angled downward at her and mouth slightly parted. Tease.

"I think you want the same thing I do. For me to take your clothes off and not do it slowly. My hands all over you and my mouth clamped to your pussy. That's what I think you want."

Her breathing quickened. She cocked her head to the side. "Is that so?"

Ty nodded. Diffused light from the consoles played with the hard lines of his face and cast his eyes in pools of shadow.

After he licked them, his lips glistened. "That's so. You want it as hard as I do. Question is, you gonna do anything about it, or you gonna let me get the ball rolling?"

He closed a bear paw of a hand over hers, raised her fingers to his lips so he could run the pad of her thumb against his bottom lip, back and forth and again before he wrapped his mouth around it. A flash of teeth made her stop breathing. "I like your taste."

She could only lick her lips in response. No words. No thoughts other than the two of them rolling around on her deck.

"I wonder what else I can taste, huh, Jackie? Your breasts? Your cunt?" The raw word was like a tiny whiplash. He'd done it on purpose too.

"Why don't you find out," she whispered, her voice shaking like the rest of her.

"A challenge?"

"An invitation."

A predatory grin stretched his mouth. Ty pinched her zipper then pulled it down. Each hook releasing sounded like tiny thunderclaps. His smell came to her, male and strong. Faint rustles from his clothes caressed her like a breeze. The whole of him—his smell, the way he sounded, his animal magnetism—fired every sense in her. Violin strings pulled to their limits. She wanted this. Had wanted it just as hard so long ago. Hadn't done anything about it. Not this time.

"Does that mean I get to take what I want?" he asked.

"I think it does."

"You *think*?"

"I *know* it does."

He wrapped a hand around her nape and hoisted her up to his face for a conquest more than a kiss. Being dunked in a volcano wouldn't have felt as hot! She shivered.

Ty's mouth captured hers, moistened lips perfect for the kind of feast she had in mind.

God, that mouth!

Growls rolled in his chest like distant thunder. Rough and demanding, his hands closed over her shoulders. She *mmm*-ed into his mouth when he crushed her to him. But he pulled away almost immediately.

"Not that I have anything against the idea of babies, but just so you know, my implant is still good for two years."

"Good to know," she replied.

Jackie was still grinning when he resumed his activity. Pawing blindly, she found the spot where he'd tucked his T-shirt into his pants, yanked high so she could snake her hands underneath and rake her fingernails all over the glorious belly, all compact and as hard as she'd imagined it'd be. Just divine. Spasms tightened his sides and pecs as she dug her fingernails in, tilled his skin.

Ty pulled his mouth away again. His eyes were dark and intense when he looked down at her. Wicked lips glistened. "Got a shower on this piece of space debris?"

"Why? You don't like the smell of a woman?"

He grinned wide. She'd worked with him for a couple of years yet never seen him smile. Not once. "I like the smell of a woman just fine. It's the stench of sweaty man that turns me off. Want to be squeaky clean if you're gonna suck my dick."

She huffed and puffed for a good two seconds while he just grinned and basked in the joy of his good comeback. "What makes you so sure I will?"

His cocky grin widened. "It's the best in the system...or so I've heard."

As much as she'd love to kick his oh-so-deserving butt, she'd more likely bite and lick it first. *Then* maybe she'd kick it. Ha.

"You're just like I remember, Terrence Weller, you arrogant ass."

"You've no idea." He trapped her mouth under his, licked then sucked her bottom lip before pulling away. "Shower, gorgeous. Lead the way."

Hands tugging each other's clothes, they barely managed the cramped passageway leading to the broom-closet-sized bathroom, complete with tiny showerhead sticking directly out of the bulkhead.

He stopped in the hatch, turned back to her then proceeded to yank his T-shirt off—muscles played under his tanned, shiny skin, rippled with loose strength over and behind his shoulders when he sent the shirt flying over her head. Even if his thighs were thick with muscles, the width of his torso still created a wide and striking V.

Ty fisted his belt buckle, froze. "You just gonna stand there and watch?"

A big smile was her reply.

With a chuckle he unclipped the belt then unceremoniously dumped his pants down around his ankles, stepped out of the wide cargo pants, boots and all. The Best Cock in the System—or so he'd boasted—bobbed in a teasing invitation when he bent over and unclipped his boots before kicking each off.

"So?" he asked. "Did I lie?"

Jackie didn't think she could answer without betraying the depth of her hormonal response to him so she just shook her head.

After he tossed everything out of the tiny cubicle, he turned away from her to work the levers and tune the shower to a nice and strong pulse. Offered her a splendid view of his tight, round butt—as tanned as the rest—and legs made for long, hard rides. Jackie leaned on the bulkhead for the simple delight of watching him move. He had maybe five minutes worth of hot water before it'd turn glacial. Her water tank had never been designed to accommodate the needs of two crewmembers.

"Care to join me?" he tossed over his shoulder as he grabbed the tube of shower gel and squirted half of it in his hand. Even this small gesture caused muscles on his wide back to ripple and cord. After he was done washing himself in brisk, economical rubs, he let the tube fall where it may. Men.

She would *not* pick it up even if the urge was strong. She enjoyed her affairs a certain way, had to keep things organized, life compartmentalized, finances balanced, had to keep juggling the many pins. Otherwise, everyone who depended on her would suffer. "I already had one."

"So?"

Before she could move out of the way, he turned, reached out of the tiny shower, closed a block-like fist over the lapel of her flight suit and yanked her inside with him.

"Hey!"

But his mouth clamping over her throat and his free hand cupping her ass quickly silenced her angry retort. The guy could do things with that mouth. She couldn't wait to see what else he could do with it.

Ty bit down on her lapel, tugged then let go. "Get rid of that before I chew through it."

"You do it," she retorted just to see a reaction.

Growling, he yanked her flight suit open then over her shoulders, tugged asymmetrically and made a mess of things as he tried to pull the wet, clingy garment down her arms. The man had such finesse...not.

"Do you need help?" she asked then teased his throat with a quick lick.

"No, but your tailor will when I'm done with the damn thing."

To put him—and herself—out of his misery, she rolled her shoulders as water made a tight mess of her clothes.

Finally she wrestled them off with Ty's enthusiastic help. With a triumphant curse, he sent it flying out of the cubicle.

"Don't move," he said, placing a large hand over her chest and pressing her back against the polymer panel. "Damn, gorgeous. *Damn*. You've any idea how hard I've wanted to see this? How bad I wanted to push you into a tight corner and have my way with you?"

His hungry gaze produced frissons up her spine as he stopped to eyeball her in a way no man had done. He didn't merely *look* at her, he *consumed* her with his hungry gaze. Jackie shivered.

"Take the rest off… I get to watch," he said, thumbing a piece of hair from her forehead.

She kicked out of her boots and soon stood in just her underwear and tank top that was plastered against her, molding her hard nipples. Water fell in rivulets out of the shower stall and spread on the bathroom floor beyond the ledge. She didn't care. Already the water was running a bit cooler.

"You forgot something." He indicated with his chin her tank top and panties. "If I do it, you might not be able to wear them again."

"What? You get carried away?"

"Not often. But for you, I'll make an exception." The glint in his eyes turned predatory. "Take them off."

She did. Because his tone thrilled her, the anticipation stimulated her. And because she *wanted to*.

Naked, she stood in front of him, close enough to touch yet neither made a move.

"Better hurry before the hot water goes," she said, wiping droplets from her face with a shaking hand. Adrenaline pumped her veins. She could hardly stand in place.

Ty leaned back against the bulkhead, offered her the rapacious grin she'd come to like—a lot—then cupped one of her breasts before rolling the nipple with his thumb.

"Nice."

Not to be outdone, she fisted his cock. God, he was hard and hot. "Nice."

With a mocking curve to his upper lip, he tightened his hold on her nipple almost to the point of pain. "*Very* nice."

She gave him a brusque pump, which tore a growl from him. "Same to you."

"You're playing with fire, Jackie."

"What makes you think I'm playing?"

A wide grin was the last thing she saw before he bent over and filled her face with his, her mouth with his. Tongue, lips, he took it all. She opened wide, curled her tongue into his mouth then sucked his bottom lip. He tasted of cinnamon and oranges.

While he kissed her, she was happy just to fill her hands with various parts of him. Just divine.

"Getting your hands full, eh?" he asked, pulling back. Manly pride and something else shone in his dark eyes. Satisfaction and...joy?

All of a sudden the water turned glacial.

Ty let out a thunderous "*Fuck!*"

Jackie squealed as she plastered herself against the side of the tight shower but couldn't go far since he'd wrapped an arm around her waist and forced her to him for a kiss that devastated her self-control and inhibitions.

While he kissed her, she felt him paw blindly along the wrong wall for the levers. She could've helped, but that would've meant taking her mouth away from his. A bit of cold – glacial – water never killed anyone. Not quickly anyway.

After a while, Ty pulled away. "How do you turn that motherfucking thing off?"

Some bit of gymnastics was needed for her to squeeze around his bulk until she stood next to the levers. She reached around him, shut the water off but yelped when he caught her arm and forced it behind her then captured the other as well. Both her wrists fit easily in one of his hands.

"Mmm, Jackie, Jackie, Jackie," he growled, gaze roaming. He leaned into her, put his mouth against her ear. "I like you this way, all curved back and ready. Like dessert. I *love* dessert. Ever licked cream off a lover's skin? Or sucked honey off a guy's dick?"

Jackie closed her eyes and enjoyed the pressure of his hand around her wrists, how his cock pressed into the junction of her thighs, so hard and hot. Ready.

"I don't have any honey on me," she taunted. "Sorry."

"Oh but you do, Jackie. You just watch me."

The pressure around her wrists changed as he pulled downward, curved her back with kisses until she'd knelt in the shower stall with her spine bent and her breasts exposed to his hungry mouth. Moaning and keeping her eyes closed, she took his licks and bites, sucks and languorous kisses as he followed her descent, bent almost in half. Looming. She loved it.

He abandoned her wrists. She felt him straighten. Something hot and silky-smooth touched her on the mouth.

"Take it," he said.

She did.

Chapter Three

ℰ

Ty could swear his toes had just curled back hard enough to touch the top of his feet. Hot damn! When her lips tightened around his cock, he almost failed at suppressing the urge to push her down on all fours and have some seriously rowdy wrestle-sex. He knew she could take it too, built like she was, all wiry strength and shoulders. Little tigress.

After a hard suck that made him hiss, he ran a hand in her hair, closed a loose fist against the back of her skull so he could sink in slowly, pull out, show her the rhythm he wanted. "You like dessert too, hmm?"

From slow and leisurely, her fist began to pump hard and fast.

Ty opened his mouth on a long, silent exhalation. "No need to rush, gorgeous. Plenty to go around."

But shit, if he didn't watch it, he'd come within the minute. Not his best performance. He couldn't believe he was having wild bathroom sex with an old crush and chief competitor. Ha! Man, he loved how Jackie's attitude matched his own. Always had. But just as he'd suspected back when they worked together, she didn't tell the whole story, let folks see the real deal. There was something more to the mouth and piloting skills. Layers that ran deep underneath the hard façade. As if she were trying to keep everyone away. What did she have to hide, he wondered. He'd never been nosy. That'd imply he cared about someone other than his baby sister and himself, which he didn't. Right?

Right.

Still, maybe he ought to scratch at Jackie's veneer, see what color showed up underneath the hard gloss. Just out of curiosity of course. Something he may be able to use later on. Not because he gave a damn. Yeah...

When she sucked particularly hard on the end of his cock, he looked down and caught her staring back up at him, one eyebrow arched. Oh prideful too, eh? Didn't want all her good work going to some guy who didn't appreciate? Well, he'd *show* her just how much he did appreciate her handling.

Before checking with her, he popped out of her mouth, grabbed her by the armpits so he could hoist her up and plant her against the bulkhead then knelt in front of her.

"You move from there," he said through a grin he knew was far from genial, "I just might spank your cute ass. Got it?"

She just snorted a very unladylike laugh and kissed the air in his direction. Fuck, he liked women with fire in them!

"You're gonna regret that, Clark."

"Bite me."

"Okay."

He did. On the inside of the thigh. She gasped and was about to smack him in the head when he caught her hand midway, reversed it then bit the inside of her wrist before placing a tender kiss on the mark. She let him do all that. He didn't scare her one bit apparently. Her, a gal alone in space— for some reason, it bugged him she'd fly courier runs without backup. He looked up at her. And as if two women were staring back down at him, he saw a duality he'd never taken the time to notice before. The hard and tender, fun and stoical, the tough pilot and warm woman.

Could she get any sexier?

Now that he looked at her, really *looked* at her, there was a third layer. Pain. He could spot pain two hundred paces away. He'd dispensed and taken quite a bit of it in his stupid years running drugs. Had it always been there, he wondered. Something recent? What?

His macho pride reared its antennas. Had a guy messed with her? Fuck, just the thought... He'd rip the jerk apart.

"What are you thinking about?" she asked. And just like that, the iceberg that was her personality sank a bit further, hid a bit deeper underneath the surface. A glimpse. Barely.

"Trying to picture you outside a pilot's chair." Keep it nice and safe. Didn't want to spook her.

Jackie smiled. "And?"

"Pretty damn hard." He kissed her belly, licked it. "You wear dresses sometimes? Short ones so your guy can take you with the thing on?"

Oh, she liked *that*.

"I love it," he went on, fanning the flames. "Fucking with clothes on."

A shiver pebbled her skin and made hard points of her nipples. He trapped one, rolled it, exulted in the moan of pleasure he triggered from her.

"Ever tried it?"

"No."

"You've had boring guys."

She shrugged. "Haven't had one of those in a while. No time."

The thought couldn't even take root in his skull. No guy in a while? Were they all fucking blind? Dumb? Both? Who wouldn't want to score a woman like her? Everyone needed someone to take the slack, to hold the light while the other fiddled under the hood. She did. He did. Everybody did. He had Lydia, who tormented him with threats of blind dates— "You're so *old*, Ty, you need a woman soon". Who did Jackie Clark have? He couldn't remember her making a single mention of family or friend. She hadn't hung out with any of the gals, hadn't dated any of the guys—he would've known right away and probably would've gotten drunk over it like the true ass he was. Had she no one? "Well, we have some now. Not much, but some."

Terrence Weller decided he wanted a whole lot more time with her. Not just a couple hours in the cramped bathroom of her ship.

"Make me a bit of room, would you?" he asked after he kissed her navel then placed another—a wet and noisy one—on her pussy. "Right here."

She hooked a foot over the shower ledge and slowly rubbed both hands downward over her belly, spread herself for him. Oh the tease. Skin shiny with water made him lick his lips. This was going to be a feast.

As soon as his mouth touched the sweet, wet cunt the color of an exotic flower, plentiful honey rewarded him.

"You were waiting for that, weren't you?"

Even though she didn't say anything, she replied with her expression. Nothing beat a woman going all dreamy at his handling.

So he gave it to her again. A wide lick. "You like that, hmm?" he mumbled against her tender flesh.

Rosy and malleable, he made her pussy his by rubbing the skin upward with his thumbs, stretching the hood off the little pearl so he could flick his tongue at it, make it all nice and tight for him. Her belly tightened then concaved. She was liking this a lot. Good girl.

"That's it, show me how you like it."

He licked her. Sucked her in deep. Repeated the actions over and over again. More honey dribbled onto his fingers. He spread the nectar then filled his face with it. Ty couldn't help the growl that sounded like a goddamn supercharged booster with no off switch. He just couldn't stop himself. He had to let the extra energy and appreciation out some way. Jackie smiled, eyes closed, bottom lip tucked between her teeth. He made her wetter than wet, then when he knew she was ready, introduced a finger into her, reversed his wrist so he could rub that special place the ladies liked. A soft moan left her.

"You like?"

"Mmyeah."

"What was that?" He rubbed her frontal wall while sucking on her clit. Oh, she liked *that*! Her hips started working. Push. Push. "I said, 'what was that?'"

She scowled, showed her teeth. "Just… Ohhh."

"Yeah," he replied through a grin. "That's what I thought."

"Don't stop," she whispered, gave his head a little smack. The clack of wet skin on skin made him grin. "Don't you *stop*."

"Or what?"

She moaned, furiously rolled her hips.

She didn't need to warn him. He didn't stop. Couldn't have. Stopping himself from eating her out wasn't something he wanted to even consider. She tasted too damn fine for starters. Like honey, salt water and something deeply feminine. A lethal cocktail. And on top of her fine taste, he loved, just *loved*, how she responded to him, how he could make her writhe and shake just with simple touches. As if he could reach through that armor she wore, the one she seemed to have built directly around herself instead of having slipped it on. Built with no closures or moving pieces in case something snuck through and hurt her. Through their sexual encounter, Ty felt as if he could touch the woman inside the armor. Using sex not as a weapon, but as a *key*.

He spotted her thighs cramping, hips working harder. She was close. Real close. Slowly, Ty introduced a second finger. Instead of licking her clit, he sucked on it. Hard.

She gasped, pulled herself up and wide for him, legs shaking, belly too. In her own little world. The wave coming, swelling. He loved watching his lovers come. Such a treat. Still, her eyes were closed. Had to change that. Had to see them.

"Look at me."

Twin black suns nearly blinded him by their intensity when she angled her chin downward. Against her skin the color of wet sand, her almond-shaped eyes resembled two shards of polished basalt. He'd seen ancient death masks with eyes like those. The passion, the quiet wisdom, the "I could kill you with my pinky but it'd mess my hair". Except hers also betrayed a great pain. Fuck, he'd give an arm to fix it. Then again, maybe he shouldn't even dare trying.

"Are you close?"

She nodded, made a soft mewling sound deep in her throat.

"How close?" He licked her pussy once, hard, then again. Pumped his fingers. "How close? Tell me."

"Close..." she whispered then bit down, lolled her head.

With his thumb he kept her nice and tight for him, sucked her clit in and used his tongue to roll it against his upper lip. Bingo.

He pulled away, growled, "Let me hear it."

"Ah... Ah... God..."

Ty felt pitiless so he continued his tongue work even though he knew she was past the point of no return. Just wanted to make sure she was going to crash through the wall, not just hit it head-on.

"That's it," he breathed over and over. Honey rewarded him in shiny ribbons. "That's it."

A gasp left him when her pussy clenched around his fingers. Damn hard too! Even the skin outside pulsed against his lips. He kissed her while she came, licked the juices that glistened on his hand and closed his eyes so he could savor the feel of her squeezing around his fingers like a wave of flesh, an adjusted sheath, a perfect home.

Something he'd never had. But the devil knew he wanted.

Jackie thought she was going to explode. Literally disintegrate into a million shards. She'd never, ever had a man eat her out with such greed before. Ever. As if he were afraid to run out, starve to death.

The violence of her orgasm both shocked and rocked her. She came and within seconds came again because he'd kept his fingers there, deep in her, his mouth clamped onto her sex, licking, sucking, kissing. Fucking.

But for the most part, it'd been his eyes. She'd been busy enjoying his handling until he'd told her to look at him. Commands had never been something she'd taken from men. Especially not in bed. She knew what she wanted and how to get it. But so did he, it would seem. Those eyes... They'd pulled her in.

No, that wasn't it. Ty had let himself into *her*. Not just physically. As if he'd been able to see inside her head, her heart, sift through the layers of defenses, somehow navigated the minefield she'd set around herself. Maybe he could tell the whole of her wasn't exactly the sum of its parts, that something was missing, a sliver that she kept all to herself. So much more perceptive than she'd given him credit.

Ecstasy rippled through her, tore a moan that emptied her lungs. The intimacy, the sharing of sensations, of their bodies, had tilted her into the abyss. And into it she still roiled now, twirling, blind, deaf, lost, like a cork on a raging sea, a leaf in a tornado, spinning and confused yet centered as never before. He did that to her, steadied her. Like a pillar. Jackie Clark needed neither security nor sheltering—she'd always provided her own—but something solid on which to lean occasionally was nice. Very nice.

She tried to reach down to caress his face, but he kept her pinned with a hand pressed against her sternum. "If you move from there I'll spank your cocky ass."

Heat flushed her cheeks. "Don't stop," she growled at him while she reached for his face again. "Just don't—"

"I warned you. Down," he snarled, pulling on her wrist. "Down on your knees."

Jackie didn't have time to protest as he pulled her to the hard deck, bent her over, torso sticking out of the stall and backend to him.

She bumped her shoulder on the door, cursed. "What the hell—"

A cry left her when he stretched her wide and shoved his face between her thighs. So this was his idea of spanking? A hot mouth then cool air provided titillating contrast. A split second after, the clack of wet-on-wet skin. Heat radiated from her butt up her back.

He'd slapped her butt? Had actually *slapped* her butt?!

"Hey!"

"Just like I thought," he whispered, bending over her to put his mouth by her ear. God, that throaty voice. "There were times I'd look at you and my hands would be tingling...*tingling*, gorgeous. Because I could imagine what it'd be like, what you'd feel like. I couldn't even think straight around you."

His voice filled her brain with vivid images at the same time as it emptied her mind of any coherent thought. All she knew was that she wanted. Everything. All of him.

"More," she whispered, chewed her bottom lip. Cut a glance over her shoulder and caught the intense look in his narrowed eyes. He positively towered over her. Muscles bulged when he shifted his weight. From whisper her voice hardened. She knew what she wanted, always had. "Give me more."

"If you ask for it, it's not a spanking, is it?"

"I won't *beg*," she retorted.

Another sound smack on the butt. A half whoop, half gasp escaped her.

"I know you wouldn't."

Tingles rippled outward from her butt to her back, which he kissed tenderly, on occasion raking his teeth over her shoulder or neck.

He slapped her butt again, lighter, more like a tap, but this time landing closer to the center. She huffed a cry, curled her spine upward. "You call that spanking?" she taunted, chuckled.

"No, that's just having fun." He pulled back, licked his way down her spine. While she watched, he knelt behind her and wrapped his big hands around her hips, thumbs digging into her cheeks. Electrifying.

"When I start," he murmured, eyebrow cocked high. The same arrogant ass — good-looking, stubborn, skilled, lovable in a gruff way — she'd enjoyed so much. "You'll know the difference, believe me."

"What are you...? Oh Jesus."

He'd just pushed his face between her butt cheeks hard enough to overbalance her and licked her in one hard pass, front to back. She shuddered, stifled a moan. Fire accompanied his mouth.

"You liked that?"

She didn't even try for smug or proud. "Yes! *Yes!*"

He brought her there again. Right against the edge. Let her breathe a couple times, let her rest. Then again. She let out a long moan. Pure torture.

"Push against me, gorgeous," he said behind her.

She did. So close. A mere touch would send her over. But instead of continuing his masterful tongue work, he proceeded to kiss her lower back, the insides of her thighs, her spine.

"Stop that," she panted. "Do what you did before."

"No."

"Come on. Dammit!"

"Next time I tell you to stay put, you going to or not?"

The wave receded. She was going to lose it. Damn him. Jackie reached between her legs to finish the job herself but he caught her wrist, planted it behind her back. Without the support, she collapsed on her side.

"That's cheating, gorgeous. Can't have that."

Before she could share with him what was on her mind, he flipped her leg up, hoisted her against him. On a long snarl, he took her. Hard and quick. She cried out his name. Maybe. She wasn't sure. All she knew was that he'd popped back out, leaving behind fever-like heat that spread wider, deeper. On a long contented moan, she came.

While she did, Jackie felt him gently rub her vulva with his glans, slowly back and forth. Fire subsided, spasms became light tingles.

"My turn for some dessert," he remarked, gave her cleft a quick tap that made her groan then stood.

"Come over here then." She patted the deck in front of her.

Grinning ear to ear, he padded around her, managed the cramped bathroom without knocking any of her things off the narrow shelves then stood with his feet—*huge* feet—wide apart, cock bobbing.

She patted the deck again.

With a roll of eyes, he went down on one knee. "You always so damn difficult in bed?"

"Only when it's good."

He seemed about to say something but just nodded, licked his upper lip when she fisted his cock and ran her palm up and down, rubbed the tip with her thumb, spread the drop of pre-cum around his glans. Into her mouth she took him. Deep. She heard his gasp, felt the shudder traverse him.

"Motherfu—" he growled.

Jackie gave him the ride of his life. With energy that bordered on frenzy, she sucked his cock as if there were no tomorrow. She rolled her fist around his shaft, licked his glans in quick little passes then slow, measured ones, tapped it against her tongue, moaned loudly as she worked her jaw to accommodate his girth. Perfect shape for her. Just wide enough, just long enough. And hot enough to burn her lips.

Ty pushed against her shoulder. "Okay, okay, goddammit. We want to keep some for later, right?"

"I don't know," Jackie replied, licking her upper lip. "Do we?"

"Oh you little…"

She yelped when he grabbed her by the crook of the hip and flipped her end to end so her butt was plastered right against his lower belly, his hands all over her breasts while his thighs nudged hers so she'd spread wider. Wild sex in her ship's tiny bathroom. Like teenagers in the back of a shuttle. The comparison made her chuckle.

"Something funny, Clark?" A trace of irritation laced his hoarse voice.

"Nope, proceed."

Without warning, he pressed his cock against her entry. Slid in all the way. She'd expected fire but couldn't be prepared for the inferno melting her from the inside out. He was so hot, so *hot*. Burning. So good. Her moan filled the tiny space. But he pulled out.

She turned, caught the look of triumph in his eyes. "Hey!"

"You want it, you're gonna have to tell me."

"I already did," she snapped as she rolled her hips back to rub herself against him. So slick and hot.

"I forgot."

The voice alone could do wonders to her libido. But Jackie still wanted what he'd taken from her. Namely his cock. "Come on, Ty. Don't tease."

"But I *love* teasing." He pushed all the way under her so their flesh rubbed in all the right places.

Fever. Cramps. Her senses rioted. "No more teasing."

The finality of her tone must have convinced him to deliver and right this instant or there'd be hell to pay.

"You're right," he said. "No more teasing."

He thrust hard and deep. Lifted her knees off the deck.

"*Ah!*"

"Again?"

"Yes! *Yes!*"

The inferno spread through her entire body. Despite the discomfort on her kneecaps, pleasure rippled along her back and thighs, down in her pussy, tightened her breasts. As if she experienced an out-of-body episode, she heard her voice rising. Ah. Ah. Ah. Ah. Crescendo, higher still. His cock filled her, stretched her, branded and claimed her. She took him in. To the end of him—of her. The wave rose. Blocked out everything else. Ecstasy hit. Fire consumed her inhibitions and alertness and reduced her to nerve endings and lungs.

Her voice was like a whip on his lower back. Ty didn't think he could give it to her any harder, deeper and with more energy than he already was. To the last ounce and inch, he imparted to her pussy the fire in his lower back and thighs, in his belly. Transferred and communicated through his body what burned him inside. Everything. Teasing lick of flames. Sensualization. Spurred by the sight of her ass jiggling for the force of his thrusts, he pounded. Pounded.

Shit. He wouldn't last long. Had already lasted a helluva lot longer than he thought possible given the serious case of fuck-fever that had descended on him. Years worth of it.

His legs burned—his balls and belly. Yet she wanted more. Yelled for it, snarled and whispered demands and threats.

A split second later he felt the wave rising. He came. Fuck, he *exploded*.

His roar surprised him. He'd never been the screamer type. But in the one second of blinding clarity, of pure ecstasy, he emptied his lungs until they burned, until his diaphragm hurt.

The world spun around his head. "Jackie..."

He tried to brace himself, failed. As if he'd been shot, he collapsed on his side, taking Jackie with him, their bodies still writhing in the throes of pleasure. Nothing mattered more than touching her, to keep touching her. Not the hard lumps under his shoulder nor the cold deck against his hip. Not the fact he'd probably lost his ship for good, nor how he was already thinking about the next time they'd have sex. He wanted there to be a next time, dammit. Wanted it and would have it.

Because in that one moment he knew, probably had known all along. She was special. Jackie Clark wasn't like any other woman out there. He'd been a damn fool for not making a move back then, and doubly a fool if he didn't latch on to her now. Ty had many faults—he was his old man's son after all, despite Lydia's claims he was a good guy trapped inside a part-time asshole—but making the same mistake twice wasn't on the list. He *never* made the same mistake twice.

* * * * *

Jackie had always enjoyed the view of Titan Five from the spaceports. Cylindrical habitats stuck on top of one another like piled logs with blue lights all around the circumference resembling bracelets of sapphires.

Sitting at her controls, she kept the station on the main viewscreen. By her side, Ty, standing, scowled still. A few minutes after uploading Ray's data from his chief designer, she'd inquired to Tower about salvage teams. Unfortunately, they were informed none would be available for weeks.

Jackie sighed. Another thing she had to fix. So many of them. Just for one day—a week was too much to ask—she'd like to lie down somewhere nice and warm and not have to organize, classify, calculate and forecast anything. Maybe even keep a weekend to herself instead of playing cards with her folks.

What the hell was she thinking?

"You okay?" he asked without turning toward her.

Jackie pinched the bridge of her nose. "Yeah. Can't wait to get home, that's all."

He straightened, tucked his T-shirt back into his cargo pants. Muscles corded enticingly on his shoulders. Despite the hours and light-years since their disorderly tryst in her bathroom, she could still feel him everywhere. "Where's home?" he asked.

"Cassiopeia, Level Four. You?"

"My ship."

Renewed guilt made her swallow hard. "I'm really —"

Ty held up his hand. "We'll figure something out. *If* your ship can take us back to Ray and his fat bank account."

Jackie couldn't help the defensive reaction. "*Lazarus* is a good ship."

"Fifty years ago, maybe."

"Hey."

Ty turned to her, rubbed his shaven skull hard. "I'm cranky right now, okay, sorry. I *need* that ship. It's Lydia's ticket, you know. Her ticket out."

"Lydia?" Her voice came out like a subdued squeak that instantly shamed her.

But it seemed to please him because he gave her one of his dark half grins. "My baby sister. She's going to be a doctor." Pride sparkled in his eyes. "She's going to make something of herself."

"I didn't know you had a sister." She didn't know the first thing about him.

Actually, she'd known *of* Terrence Weller for years. Had thought she had him figured out. A driven courier, a skilled pilot, a man too hot to touch. But Jackie realized now she hadn't understood the first thing about him, that a depth of character lurked beneath the rough shell, the badass attitude. He was still the big scary guy with whom no colleague had wanted to fly. But a sensitive streak ran through him. A sliver of blue sky between thunderclouds.

"She's twenty, studies at the Reykjavik School of Medicine, back on Earth where we're from."

"That's a very prestigious school," Jackie replied with a nod. Must cost a fortune. She was shocked a courier could afford the tuitions alone, never mind the residency programs and cost of living on Earth. Ty must have been sending three quarters of his earnings down that way. Not unlike her. The age difference between the siblings also surprised her. Ty was at least in his mid-thirties.

"Lydia surprised *all* of us," he said with a tight smile. "I was sixteen when she was born, so I was old enough to see the storm coming. I took care of her when my folks finally split. It'd been years in the making, so no big shock. I did what my old man should've done, made sure she had a clear shot at a good life, properly beat up her first boyfriends, that sort of things."

She smiled. "The best part of a big brother's job, I'm sure."

"Damn right. Plus, if you're not there for those in your family who deserve it," he said with a shrug, "what the hell good are you to anyone?"

Jackie's heart skipped a beat.

Her reaction to his comment must have surprised—and intrigued—him since he faced her, cocked his head. "Is that why you were always pulling double shifts, why you're running the belt nowadays? Need the extra credits? You're taking care of someone?"

"No."

Those were her affairs. Not anything she wished to share. Before she could weasel out of the situation, he turned his attention to the consoles. Jackie suspected he'd done it on purpose and was thankful for it.

"What's going on now?" he remarked, pointing at the rising numbers on the temperature dial. "We're not even off Titan Five and your ship's overheating?"

"*Lazarus* is always within that range. It's normal."

"For you it is," he grumbled, crossed his arms. Jackie yawned, sat straighter at the console then maneuvered *Lazarus* out of the docking station, computers full of Ray's data, and soon, her coffers full of his credits. It'd taken her a bit longer than usual to reach Titan Five, download the data, fuel up then get ready to head back home. They'd hit a traffic jam minutes before reaching the station's airspace. A backup of ships worth ninety minutes because of solar activity at the edge of the system messing with transmissions. Waste of time. But what a ride it'd been. In every sense of the word.

"You gonna answer that?" he grumbled.

She snapped out of her mental trip to find the nav console bleeping at her. "Reports indicate heightened solar activity," a female Tower said after Jackie activated the link. The voice sounded like her Aunt Flora's. Nasal, annoying but well-meaning. "All ships are advised to stay in port."

"Copied, *Lazarus* out," Jackie replied then cut the comms. She didn't need Aunt Flora to fly her run back home. She knew the way with her eyes closed. Half closed.

"You always fly blind?" Ty asked, coming to stand right over her shoulder. The heat of his body close to hers scattered her neurons. "She just said there was solar activity, something's going on. A storm probably. Tune on the news so we can see what's up."

"It's just some solar activity, not a full-fledged storm. Otherwise she wouldn't have just 'advised' us to stay. We have time to make it to Cassiopeia."

"Still, I wanna know what the hell's going on." He reached over her shoulder for one of the smaller viewscreens, froze midway. "Old habits," he said a few inches from her ear. "Not my ship."

Heat flared out of her suit. God, would she ever get used to that throaty voice? "That's...um, that's okay." Still, that he'd ask first pleased her.

After a long, sexually charged look that made her hot and ready for more—no time, dammit, they had a run to do—he tuned the comms to Titan Five's civilian channel, which filled the slate-gray panel with first static then images of a newsroom.

"You think they have dirty movies on?" His chuckle raised the hairs on her arms. "Maybe we could make our own, hmm?"

"Then sell them for profit...or not."

A frisson tightened her nape when Ty leaned closer, put his mouth right against her ear. His scent filled her nose, her brain. He smelled like man. "How 'bout I spank your cocky ass here and now, hmm? Bend you over that console right there? You think we'd make profit on *that*?"

With meaning plain on his face, he licked his hand from palm to fingertips, slapped his thigh. Despite the cargo pants, the clack reverberated once. In spite of herself, she started. Prickling like hot needles poked her along the inside of the thighs. That could've been her butt. It *had* been her butt only a couple of hours ago. A spike of adrenaline and thrill shot down her spine. He could make her hot with just a few whispered words and a cheap trick. It was that throaty voice! And the hot body, and the attitude, and... Yeah, well, the whole package.

His pupils and nostrils dilated when she leaned away from him so she could stare fully into his face. "Are you making me a promise or a threat?"

"Which one would piss you off the most...*gorgeous?*"

Had she been hooked to medical machines right now, her blood pressure would've broken records. Wasn't all bad either. "Oh you big—"

An image on the news caught her attention. A reporter was interviewing a woman in a white HAZMAT suit tied at the waist. White for medical situations, Jackie remembered. Orange meant industrial.

The images mixed with those of another "expert" six years before in a likewise white HAZMAT suit, telling everyone that Nova Luna colony airspace had been sealed, trapping everyone inside. And aid *outside.*

Jackie remembered even now, years later, the exact feeling in her gut when she'd realized her parents had just shuttled relief workers to the site. The sinking, the downward spiral. Then it'd been fighting all the red tape, the waiting, the excruciating pain of watching her parents' ruined bodies on gurneys in the halls of overcrowded hospitals when governments had allowed the sick off Nova Luna. Crushing bills. Humiliating insurance questionnaires that wanted details no one should share.

Above all, the fear that should something happen to her, the only child, her parents would not only live in medicated misery but in wretched poverty as well.

Jackie's eyes stung as she looked away, cleared her throat.

"Doesn't look good," Ty remarked. Even if he wasn't looking at her, she knew he was watching her reaction.

She tried not to give him any. Failed.

"What's wrong?"

"I'm good. Just tired."

"Being tired doesn't make you look like you've seen ghosts, Jackie. It makes you dull, stupid, slow. Cranky, in my case. But not the way you look now."

"I said I'm *okay*," she snapped.

For a long time Ty just watched her as a hawk would, leaning over the console, gaze intent on her face as if he waited. For what, she didn't know, wanted to believe she didn't care either. Such a lie. She cared what he thought. In fact, she'd developed something of a small crush on him. Too bad she didn't have the time to do anything about it. She couldn't let him see inside. That was for her alone. Not something to share with a man—a competitor, for God's sake!

Breathe, she mentally scolded.

"If you say so," he said at length, straightening.

If he had raged and complained, cursed or acted like a frustrated macho, it would've been easier to deal with. Jackie was used to those reactions, had become adept at fighting the pushy, straight-arming through doors. What she hadn't dealt with before was a man—especially one like the "scary" Ty Weller, who had terrified other couriers—to show such empathy and restraint. Such understanding and patience.

"I'm okay," she repeated, calmer. "I don't like these things, I don't like how they're dealt with, you know. All the damn red tape while folks suffer."

He nodded, eyes narrowed pensively as he turned the screen off.

Prox alerts bleeping saved her from trying to claw her way out of the hole into which she'd let herself slide. Again. The asteroid belt and the gas giant loomed in front of her prow. Still light-years away but already menacing. She had to snap out of it.

"Okay," she said. "Here we go."

They were about to enter the dangerous part of their journey back and she needed all her faculties intact. As much as the haunting images of both tragedies allowed.

Jackie tried to keep the positive in mind. Within hours she'd have her account full of credits.

And Terrence Weller wouldn't have a single thing. No ship, no livelihood. His baby sister may not become a doctor after all. Maybe he'd feel the way she would if she could no longer afford the private sanitarium where her folks resided. Damn.

She sighed. But what else could she do? She'd already taken him onboard, promised to help with the salvage. What *more* could she do?

"What do you say I man the nav side while you fly this old clunker?"

"I don't need —"

"Did I ask if you needed help?" he snapped. "No. I said you mind if —"

"Yeah, yeah, sure. You man the nav. If it'll help you shut up, do it."

He kissed the pad of his middle finger, extended it to flip her the bird then blew the "kiss" toward her. "Don't turn me on, gorgeous, I can't focus when I'm turned-on."

She snorted a laugh. How could he do this? Make everything just blink out? As if the two of them on her flight deck were her entire universe?

He grinned wide when she shook her head, made room for him to work the nav console by her right. Frankly, in her condition, sleep-deprived and fighting the effects he had on her, she didn't mind his help flying through the dreaded asteroid belt, especially since a thick cluster of building-sized rocks was coming at them hard and fast. Millions of tons of silicate, iron and other hard things that made space ships go *crunch*. Yet she wouldn't have it any other way. Those were the runs that paid the best.

"Okay, we're there," she said. Excitement made her voice high-pitched.

Five thousand miles off her prow, the asteroid belt's outer ring, populated with smaller chunks. Every last one still big enough and hard enough to pulverize *Lazarus*.

"It's turning you on," Ty murmured, licked his upper lip. "We've got a hail of incoming boulders and you're getting wet. Damn, you're something else, Jackie Clark."

She took the compliment for what it was and reciprocated with a provocative eyebrow wiggle that seemed to momentarily make him lose his focus. The lump in his cargo pants also betrayed his state of mind.

"When this is over..." he said. His feral expression finished the statement.

Jackie shivered. When this was over...

"Heads up," Ty went on, all business as he stared hard at the console over which he stood. No co-pilot chair. Never intended to *have* a co-pilot in the first place. Not that she disliked the idea of backup though, even if at first she'd hated the notion of relinquishing that much control over her schedule. Losing control meant delays, loss of profit, more problems with which she'd have to deal. "Starboard, two thousand miles. A big one."

Big indeed.

She knew stations smaller than this baby. Damn. She fired the thrusters at half capacity, cleared the Big One, as Ty had justly dubbed it, only to meet its family trailing behind. A veritable cloud of them.

"We need to get the hell out of here," she announced before gunning the engines for three seconds. A full burst that pressed her into the seat. By her side, Ty grabbed one of the rods holding the viewscreens in place and used it as a Holy Shit Handle, held on while he kept working navigation with his free hand.

"There's a clear spot two point one miles wide," he said. "Gonna be tight."

"Heading?"

"Eleven o'clock."

"Hang on."

"With your fine piloting, damn right I'm hanging on."

She laughed as she entered into a lazy spin, cleared the massive cluster of asteroids, her left wing coming within hundreds of feet of the closest one. Close. The prox alerts concurred with that. She silenced them. Damned screaming banshees.

"You know what Russian roulette is?" he asked without taking his gaze off his work.

Jackie banked left, leveled off. A quarter burst then attitude jets at full capacity. "No. What's that?"

"Folks used to play it. Half a mile, portside, nice and steady, that's it. Put a bullet in the chamber and spin it, point the gun to your head then see if you're lucky. Damn, you came close!"

"You think that's close?"

Just as she cleared the last asteroid, the milky white and smoky blue gas giant's curvature, all thirty-seven thousand miles of it, allowed for a look at its lower orbit. A flash of silver caught her attention. Guilt stabbed her deep. She recognized that shape, the silvery hull.

Ty's crippled ship.

Chapter Four

Just as when she'd watched the news, her expression changed from the tough-as-nails pilot who could make his balls cramp with just a look, to what he was presently seeing. A wounded soul.

The same pain he'd glimpsed when they'd had sex...though not just a glimpse now. Pain and something else — fear? What could possibly frighten the toughest woman he knew? But she *was*. He could tell. Something frightened her to the core. Of course, his macho side decided he should fix that right this instant and damn the torpedoes.

"Hey," he said gently. "You all right?"

She shook her head, pointed to a spot near the upper right corner of the screen. "Your ship." Her voice was subdued.

He took a look at the screen. Tensed.

"Yeah," he snarled, taking his gaze off the screen before he popped a vein. "That's my ship all right."

She'd royally screwed him, hadn't she? In every sense of the word. He should be mad at her. Which he was. Hell, he should be mad*der*. Lydia's semester was ending, which would give him barely three months to find enough money for her residency placement in the fall. Fuck. Maybe he'd have to do the kind of runs that had landed his ass in trouble back in his stupid years. Hell no. There had to be another way.

"I'm sorry, Ty," Jackie said with a quick look his way. "I really am. I'll make it up to you, okay?"

Sleeplessness stung his eyes, made him ornery as all hell. "Just fly the damn thing, would you? I'll figure something out. I always do."

"It's my mess."

"Oh what, now we're going to argue for whose fault it is the most? For fuck's sake!"

Thing was, he didn't feel the rage he ought to. Why the fuck wasn't he enraged at Jackie's little stunt? She'd cost him his ship. He wouldn't get the agreed-upon cut. Plus, he'd have to mount a salvage run, hire someone, the works. It'd take days, weeks. But he'd make sure Jackie Clark defrayed some of it. Her fault, after all. Fucking right.

He cut a glance down at her, the way she sat hunched over the control stick, white-knuckled fist around it, thumb ready to fire the boosters, feet on the pedals, eyes on the target. A study in determination. A picture of focus. And in his book, the cutest chick he'd ever met, just as he'd thought when they worked together years ago.

What had she done to him? Crippled his ship and male ego as thoroughly as she had wormed her way into his head. He should *hate* her for half of what she'd done, potentially crippled Lydia's future. But he didn't and that was that.

In fact, he was starting to like her a lot, despite the bristly carapace—or probably *because* of it.

Already he was getting a hard-on just remembering what they'd shared. Never mind what the future held in store. Because he *did* intend to spank her ass good, give the cocky little shit her due. He'd love every second of it.

After a colorful curse—that could be done to goats?—Jackie checked her watch, grimaced. There was plenty of time left to reach Cassiopeia Station, why did she look as if they were out? She muttered something he didn't quite catch, leaned closer to her workstation. Then out of the blue, changed headings, aimed straight for the planet.

WTF?

He spread his feet wider for the change in velocity. The woman needed another damn seat on this old clunker. "Hey! What the hell are you doing?"

"Watch our back," she replied.

"Where the *fuck* are you going?"

"I always clean up my own messes."

"And that's supposed to tell me what? Six o'clock, right on our tail." He gritted his teeth when she cleared the asteroid with a powerful burst of boosters and a deft roll that made his innards churn.

She turned to him. And he knew.

"You're *nuts*," he breathed, half awed, half disbelieving.

She didn't intend to...

A roll of the eyes, another inspired curse. "I *am* nuts."

"You can't do that," he growled, shook his head. "Hell, even *I* can't do that."

"I am...correction, *we* are." Eyes like twin dark suns stared right into his heart and soul.

It'd been more than a crush he'd had on her. Denial wouldn't work anymore.

"Fuck!"

Like a bullet, she shot straight for lower orbit, prow dead center as though she meant to fly right through the gas giant — which she couldn't do of course. But the aim was the same. Within seconds, the asteroid belt was behind them and every system on the old ship was bleeping, wailing, chiming their little hearts out as she fought against the planet's gravitational pull. His nav aids indicated they had to either level off or become a hunk of burning metal on their way to a fiery death.

"You intend to kill us quick or slow?"

"You're not afraid, are you?" Despite the bravado, he could see fear in her gaze, in the way a muscle twitched along her jaw.

"Nah," he replied, hiking his belt buckle higher. "Just wanna make sure you know what you're doing."

They exchanged a smile and a nod. If they came out of this alive, he was taking the woman out on a proper date before fucking their respective brains out.

Feet wide, hands on the only thing he trusted could take his weight, Ty licked his bottom lip, let out a curse just to take the edge off. "Did I ever tell you I love crazy women? Always have."

She didn't reply, only kept flying toward the very, very large planet. It was kind of pretty, now that he had all the luxury in the world of staring at its blue, purple and green roiling surface. On the main viewscreen, the planet grew, filled every pixel. At the upper right corner, growing as well, his ship. Goddamn, she really was going through with this.

"Jackie," he started, shook his head when she pulled on the control stick, executed a hellishly tight hairpin that made him feel as though he weighed four hundred pounds. Fuck, he wanted a seat already!

"Even if you retrieve my ship, there won't be enough time to make it back to Cassiopeia," he finished.

"I know."

"You realize what it means."

"I do."

So she *had* changed. He'd never known Jackie Clark to do anything for free.

"Even if it's all your fault," he said, grinning when she threw him a quick, murderous glance. "I'll make it up to you. How 'bout steak and sex? My treat, both."

"Terrence Weller, you guide me through this next run, and I swear it'll be a date you'll always remember. Now you're my eyes."

And her willing sex slave, but that he didn't say out loud. Had to preserve some bit of dignity, right? It was enough he felt all choked up over her crazy stunt. She was one in a million, and if he had his say, all his.

Sweat trickled down her temple as she licked her lips, gave little jerks to the joystick to bring them in gradually—or as gradually as one could flying a ship to rendezvous with another while in low orbit. Twenty miles. Fuck, the planet was pulling them in hard.

"Forty-five degrees, forty-four, forty. You know that spanking... I wasn't yanking your chain. You're getting one."

"Already did."

"Then you're getting another."

She laughed. "Bring it on."

He'd never been so damn turned-on. He could die in the next minute. They could crash into his ship, or miscalculate and nosedive toward the planet, the ship could disintegrate within minutes, seconds, but he had never been so turned-on in his entire life. Jackie Clark had gotten under his skin. And he guessed she'd snuck into another tight spot as well...his heart.

Well, wouldn't Lydia enjoy tormenting him now!

"Ten miles," Ty warned. If his face became any tighter, it'd crack down the middle.

She could relate. She was basically going against every pilot instinct and training, every trait of human nature. No one had ever attempted what she—*they*—were about to do. Recover a ship in low orbit without the benefit of tractor hooks and a salvage team. A ship-to-ship operation. Nuts. Crazy. Suicidal. And the one option in the repertoire of choices that didn't make her feel as if she were taking the wrong turn in her life. She *had* to get Ty's ship back, right the wrong she'd done. She *had* to do it.

"Nine! Damn, Jackie...eight, seven."

She readied her mooring clamps. A deep *thunk* indicated they'd extended out of her ship's underbelly, ready to latch on. If she missed by a lot, she'd send both ships twirling toward the gas giant looming in the viewscreen. If she missed by a little, she'd puncture his ship or it'd rip her own hull, sending everyone to the pearly gates with their guts in their hands. If she didn't miss, maybe, just maybe, they stood a chance of making it back to Cassiopeia alive. But not on time. Ty had judged right—there wouldn't be time to reach the station and upload the data to Ray's account. Not a chance in hell. She'd blown a run for the first time in her career, and how did it make her feel? Turned-on and proud. And that was that.

"Tell me when it's five and a half," she snapped. Sweat seeped into her eyes. She angrily wiped it off with her wrist.

He must have understood her plan—if she could call it that—since by the corner of her eye, she saw him nodding. He bent closer over the console, kissed the top of her head. "If you kill us, I'll kick your ass. But thanks all the same."

"I told you." She killed both fore attitude jets and aft thrusters. "I clean up my own messes. Always have."

"I said stop it, you're giving me the fuck-nows." He cursed, hand hovering near the controls, knowing that when she gave the signal, he'd have to work quickly and give her a split-screen visual.

Jackie blew air through pursed lips. Her heart beat so hard it hurt.

"Six miles," Ty snarled. "Five point seven five, five point five, point two five...five miles!"

"Now!"

Ty deftly switched to split screen to give her a close-up of the ships' underbellies while keeping the main view on screen...in case they wanted to see the planet coming.

With a grunt, Jackie pulled on the control stick so her prow would rise, offering her belly to Ty's crippled ship, slowing down to its speed and hopefully—with a lot of luck—fly alongside long enough for the clamps to latch on to the other's hatch.

A godawful metal-against-metal noise made her teeth rattle. Ty cursed. She did as well. A loud *clang* and the smell of smoke filled the flight deck, immediately sucked out by the emergency systems.

Ty leaned over the screen. "Half a foot...closer... Now!"

Since he had the nav aids, she trusted his timing and judgment and activated the mooring clamps just as the two ships flew perfectly aligned, belly to belly.

Even if this run would set her back several months — she'd have to fly at least eighty hours a week for a month — it'd also pay her in ways different than mere credits. It felt *right*. She was doing the right thing to the right person. He'd said himself if one wasn't there for those deserving help, then one wasn't worth much. Jackie believed in it. If she didn't help Ty get his ship back, after she'd crippled it, what sort of courier would she be? And what sort of woman? She'd worry about the financial consequences after. But one thing was for sure, she wouldn't have trouble sleeping or looking at herself in the mirror. There was just so far she was willing to take her tough-chick persona.

"Power up," he warned. "*Hurry*, gorgeous."

Jackie gave her old ship the ride of its life. She'd never asked of her engines what she presently demanded of them — not only to tear out from low orbit, but to tow another, larger ship behind as well. But it did. *Lazarus*, all engines at maximum and entering the red zone, gradually put distance between its aft and the gas giant.

But they weren't out of trouble yet. They had to actually clear the last few light-years of asteroids before breathing a sigh of relief.

"Dead-on," Ty warned. "Two miles. Coming in fast."

She banked a bit earlier than she would've normally since she towed another ship. Perfect timing. The large chunks of death-by-pulverization harmlessly spun by their right wing.

"Well, I'll be damned," Ty said, clearly awed. "This old thing's got some life left in it."

She patted the armrest, grinned. "You did good, babe."

"Thanks, you didn't do too bad yourself."

Jackie rolled her eyes as she turned to Ty. "I was talking to *Laz*—"

The grin on him would power a station. His eyes sparkled. "You know I'm killing my badass rep for you, grinning like an idiot. If I ask for a tissue, just shoot me."

She matched his grin. "That date—when do you want it?"

The grin turned feral, the eyes blazing. "The hull will still be warm when I tear your clothes off and have my way with you. And oh, bring some honey, if you have any. I mean the kind that comes in tubes."

"Honey?"

"Yeah," he whispered, licked his upper lip. "Ho-ney."

Before her heart could regain its normal rhythm, his expression switched to business. "Cassiopeia?" he asked, fingers poised over the controls.

She gave him a quick nod because she didn't think she could use her voice yet.

Behind her, the burst pipe whistled. Things couldn't be better. In fact, right now with the man who kept calling her "gorgeous", the man on whom she'd had a bit of a crush years before, and her ship rapidly overheating, she realized her life was all right. All right indeed.

* * * * *

"What'd he say?" Ty asked as Jackie joined him on the flight deck of his crippled ship. He had weeks of repairs to look forward to. The dead of space had that effect on ship interiors.

He'd showered and shaved, changed into crisp white coveralls and none had toned down the primal, rough edge to him. A mix of rugged, outdoorsy guy and rowdy bar doorman. She loved the duality in him, always had. In portholes the size of house bay windows, Cassiopeia Station gleamed like the silver gem it was. Two hundred feet below, workers in dark blue uniforms milled along the spaceport. In a small viewscreen near the deckhead, he'd tuned to visual-only news, which showed the same haunting footage as they'd seen back at Titan Five. Jackie tried not to look at it. She didn't want to deal with his questions.

"Let's just say," she said with pretend levity, "Ray won't be calling either of us to courier his data runs. Not for a long time."

"Fuck," he snarled, shaking his head. "Best goddamn run I've ever done and still don't get a single fucking credit. That just burns my ass."

Jackie nodded, leaned on the fancy console. High tech, like the rest of Ty's ship.

She'd broken the agreement, had docked that morning and uploaded the data four hours too late, which had cost Ray the new spaceport contract for the station being built just off the nebula. He'd been *livid*. She wouldn't get a single credit, he'd yelled over the comms. Not a damn one. His accent had thickened to the point where she hadn't been too sure just *what* language he was speaking. It all meant the same to her—no two point six mil.

"How bad is the damage?" She tried not to look as sorry as she felt. One second of reckless idiocy and an entire row of dominoes had come tumbling. Not that it was all bad, considering the outcome. Both alive. Both ships relatively intact.

But both scrambling to find funds for their respective needs and responsibilities. Not her brightest moment.

"It's bad," Ty replied, grunted a curse as he peeled a piece of brittle vinyl off the backrest. The implacable cold of space had frozen it, causing cracks all over the smooth, black finish. Just his seats alone were worth a fortune each. And he had two of them. Maybe she should consider adding one, just in case...

"Anything that can't be fixed?"

He shrugged. His massive shoulder pulled at the white coveralls. The thing wasn't sexy in the least—on anyone else—but it still made her tight and twitchy. Her palms tingled.

"Everything can be fixed, when you look at it from all angles," he said after rubbing the back of his shaven head. "Anything important, anyway."

She agreed with a small nod.

"What about you?" He snapped his chin in the general direction of her ship, which was moored somewhere in front of his. "Lost anything?"

"I'm not sure. Maybe I gained something."

There she was again, her expression turning dark and sad. Pained. What did she hide? Why the hell did she think she ought to carry all that crap—whatever it was—by herself? She was more macho than he was, for fuck's sake!

On the screen showing the news, he caught a short video of Red Star humanitarian ships waiting hull to hull, moored four deep and three abreast. Below the giant silvery hulls, he could recognize Mars' docks. A cluster fuck to fly at the best of times. He could just imagine the mess whatever was happening had caused.

Which brought him back to her expression. She watched the video as if part of her would rather chop her hand off. He'd offer to turn it off, but decided against it. Not this time. He was getting to the bottom of this. He hated to see her suffer this way.

"So," he said in his most teasing voice, the one he reserved for his favorite tigress. "All dressed up like that, you trying to turn me on so you can sneak in a sucker punch?"

She'd ditched the flight suit and instead wore a sexy white cotton shirt and beige cargo pants that did wonders to his imagination. A nice sturdy belt just the way he liked. Made a perfect handle for a disorderly go against the wall.

With a sigh, she turned her gaze to him. Remnants of the mysterious pain still lingered in her gaze. "No. Look, I'm sorry my little stunt cost you so much. I acted like an idiot."

Well, damn. Was that a crack he saw in her armor? There was an actual woman under all the titanium plating?

"Did that hurt, gorgeous? I bet it did. But thanks all the same."

He hooked his index finger at her, wanted to reel her in with the force of his gaze alone. She crossed the distance between them.

"Did you bring any?"

"Bring what...? Oh damn. The honey. Sorry, I didn't think— Well, I thought it wouldn't be for—" She blushed. Actually *blushed*.

Ty tsk-tsked, shaking his head. "I knew you'd forget." He slipped his hand in his pocket, produced a narrow, golden tube. He'd found it while rummaging around his galley, where the content of the cupboards littered the deck. Space was a bitch on ship interiors. "You women think guys never plan ahead. See, I did. Actually," he looked around, shrugged, "repairing my ship wasn't even on my mind. This *was*."

He stared holes into her shirt as he leaned over, put his mouth by her ear and waited, immobile, gauging. Baiting. He didn't say anything at first, just let his lips hover near her lobe then lower against that spot right under her jaw. She smelled like soap and woman. "You know what I think, Jackie Clark?" he whispered.

"What?" Her breathing sounded labored. He grinned. Just perfect for what he had in mind.

"I think," he whispered, nibbled her lobe then licked her neck. She tasted so good. Smelled even better. He loved everything about her. "I think you've wanted this for a long, long time."

She agreed with a quick nod.

"So have I. I'd fuck other women, but it was you I'd be thinking about. I'd compare and bitch to myself, I'd fill my face with their pussy all the while burning for my little Asian tigress. You have any idea what it does to a guy? Not getting what he wants? Turns them into motherfucking lunatics."

Ty circled her waist with an arm then grabbed her butt cheek. It fit his palm perfect. He was getting hard enough to hurt. Man, the effect she had on him. "I showed you mine, you know I've had it in for you since day one. Now you have to show me yours." He tried not to growl the last few words but failed.

"It was your voice," she said through her teeth. He felt her take a long intake of air. "Man, that voice, Ty... It could do things to me."

Pride would make his head too big to fit in doorways. "Like what?"

"Make me sigh, make me wet."

"Are you now?"

"Yes."

"Which brings us back to this," he whispered, holding the tube at chin level as he pulled away. "I thought I'd wait for a proper date, but fuck it, life's too short to wait for every damn last zero to align. What d'you think? You want to wait?"

If she shook her head any harder, she'd worry him.

He unscrewed the cap, reversed it to pierce the tube's metal membrane. A golden pearl pushed out. He let her see it before bringing the tube up against her bottom lip. She licked the golden drop off.

He pulled away by a step so he could see her better. "If I told you to take your shirt off, would you?"

A nod. Quick and firm. No hesitation there.

Ty made a conscious effort to not stop breathing. "Take it off."

Hands shaking, she unbuttoned her shirt then shrugged it off. The cotton made a soft rustling sound as the garment crumpled to the deck. Her skin around the white camisole shone and looked freshly creamed. Nipples tented the slinky fabric. No bra? His palms tingled.

She stood proud and strong, the tough cookie and brazen pilot, held his gaze. The iceberg had once again sunken underneath the surface. He wouldn't let her carry it all by herself. Too much for one person. He was there, wanted to help, meant to stick around for the long run if she let him.

"Do you like it when your guy looks at you while you're taking your clothes off?"

"I haven't had that sort of time lately."

"Why not? What's more important than this?" He gestured at her from head to toe. "I'd let nothing get in the way of this."

A half-resigned, half-defiant expression tightened her face. Clearly, there was a battle going on beneath the surface. "I have people who need me. It takes a lot of my free time."

"People? What, you got a tribe somewhere waiting for the huntress to bring back the bacon?"

Jackie snorted a laugh, shook her head. "My parents."

Ty logged the small victory then gave her that crooked grin he knew she liked. "Are you cold?"

"No, why?"

"Then you can take that off too." Jackie slipped the camisole over her head, dropped it on the deck between them. Not a stitch of rebellion. They both wanted the same thing.

His balls cramped painfully. He was turned-on like never before. But he had to get inside that armor. He didn't mind using the moment. Ty refused, just *refused* to let her stew in whatever was bringing her down. He liked her too much.

When he approached, he almost popped a vein just watching her nipples grow gradually harder-looking and tight.

Goose bumps pebbled her belly and shoulders. Ty tucked his bottom lip in, bit down hard so he could keep his cool while he dropped a single pearl of honey on one of her collarbones, let it slowly make its way down to her breast. Her belly quivered. Oh he had her now.

Without giving her time to process the movement, he leaned into her abruptly, gave her breast a quick, hard lick. He heard her grind her teeth, let a soft moan out through the nose.

"Your folks are lucky to have a daughter like you who takes care of them."

"T-They took care of me...oh God, do that again. They did it for me. It's my turn."

He pressed another drop of honey on the same breast, licked it again, trapped the nipple so he could flick his tongue underneath it, even allowed himself a bit of teeth action. Not hard.

"I don't have a brother or sister," she murmured. He saw her close her eyes, let her head loll back. The skin of her throat looked too damn tempting to ignore. He licked her in a long, slow pass. "I'm all they have."

"They're older, are they?" Honey in that dip between the collarbones. A series of little bites upward. She shook from head to feet.

"No, they're—" She stopped abruptly.

Ty wanted to curse. More honey then? No problem. She arched into him when he applied a bead of golden torture to each of her nipples. Ty could swear he'd drop dead on the deck if his heart beat any faster, any harder. But he fought the primitive urges to bend her over and take her. He wanted her to do it first. She had to let him in on many different levels.

Jackie sighed. "They're ill, very ill."

Tongue and lips against her throat, he set the tube on the console behind her so he could fill his hands with her butt, squeeze it, use it as an anchor to hoist her in against him, bend her back.

"Something recent?" he asked between kisses to her nipples.

"Six years ago. They were on Nova Luna."

Oh shit.

A wave of sympathy choked him as suddenly and as powerfully as if someone had tied a noose around his neck and yanked on it. Nova Luna was where a vicious killer disease had wiped out almost everyone on either end of the age spectrum. The very young and very old hadn't been able to fight it. Her folks must have been built from tough stock to survive the disaster that had closed the colony down and cost the elected government a few fistfuls of feathers for their handling of it. Dragging their feet didn't begin to apply.

"That's why you quit your job," he murmured, understanding dawning on him. "That's why you had to leave."

He could just imagine how a professionally driven and proud woman must have felt leaving her life behind to take care of ailing parents. She'd done it without hesitation and now obviously held no rancor. As he'd told her, if one weren't there for those in one's family who deserved it, one wasn't worth shit. In his book, Jackie Clark fucking *rocked*!

"Ah!" He'd bitten her breast, not hard but obviously enough to thrill. "Yeah, I had to. Had to be close. Spent days camped in my ship waiting to go...they wouldn't open the airspace." Anger hardened her voice.

"They didn't want more people getting sick."

"No!" she snapped. "That's not it at all. They were just trying to buy time—at the expense of those on Nova Luna—so the authorities could spin the news. Hide their shame and their mistakes."

"Like what?"

"I don't want to talk about it."

Ty abandoned her butt to gather her breasts, which he squeezed and molded, to her obvious delight, rolled the nipples against his thumbs, gave quick little licks. "What, they dragged their feet? They didn't process visas quick enough?"

"The airspace!" she growled, kicked the deck. "They closed the airspace too soon, damn them! I was there! Right *there* in orbit!"

Terrence Weller had never shied away from anything or anyone. And he wouldn't now. When something *had* to be done, it had to be done. But damn, it'd hurt both of them.

"They sealed the place too soon or you got there too late?"

Jackie froze.

"You asshole!"

Ty wasn't quick enough to parry the first punch to the snout but when the second came a split second after, he was ready. With the taste of blood on his tongue, he grabbed her just as she swung for a right hook that would've done some damage to his good looks and yanked her to him. But she fought him. Good God she fought him. Knees in the crotch, remaining fist flying. She spat curses and threats.

"What the hell do you mean, too late?!" she cried, trying to squeeze out. "What's that supposed to mean?!"

"Is it why there's always this cloud following you around? Huh?"

"Fuck you! I don't owe anyone anything!"

Ty cursed when she managed to slip an arm out of his wrist lock and landed another punch, this one in the solar plexus. He *oomph*-ed and quickly used his weight to pin her against the console ledge.

"Yes, you do," he growled back. "You owe it to yourself to toss that baggage. There's no need for any of that shit."

"Shit?" she snarled. "You're calling my life and my choices 'shit'?"

As tough and as strong as she was, she just couldn't fight gravity and the laws of nature. It must have burned her ass, but she couldn't dislodge him. For a terrible moment, Ty used every parcel of strength and every fiber of muscle to make a cage of himself around her, a frame within which she could rage and vent, curse and rile against everything.

Why couldn't she have arrived earlier, she asked through a snarl. Who'd take care of them if something happened to her? Who did they have but her? What made it okay for the authorities to close the airspace knowing they'd just added to the death toll? How could she keep going at the rate she did, juggling more and more pins? Why did he do this to her? Did he hate her? Had she done something to him?

For a terrible moment, he took within himself the hurt, confusion, despair, guilt and hatred. He took the fear as well. All into him.

Sweating and shaking—the woman could *kick*—he felt her grow limp in his arms. Then start to tremble. He closed his eyes and took that as well. The tears.

Jackie hadn't cried so hard since she'd first learned of her parents' fate. Hell, she hadn't even cried that hard *then*. Damn Terrence Weller. She hated him.

The thought stopped her cold.

She didn't hate him. How could she? She now realized what he'd done. She knew she wouldn't have let him in any other way, that she was much too proud and stubborn to let someone just waltz in. He'd had to use other means, trick her. With the best of intentions. Knowing she could push him away for good. He cared enough to try to help. God knew she never let anyone even *try*. But Ty had forced her to let him in. She *could* hate him. Maybe should. Chose not to. Life was all about choices, wasn't it? This rough man, this big, scary guy who'd always intimidated her had a gentle streak inside, a kind and generous angle—a great older brother and now a dear friend to her—to the hard rest of him.

Sweat and tears linked them. In their struggle, he'd kept his cheek plastered against her forehead, his muscled arms around her to pin hers, had even managed to squeeze in a thigh between hers. God knew she'd landed a few good kneecaps in his crotch. And some punches. He'd stayed there for who knew how long as she'd thrashed and fought. It was gone now. The fight, the rage. She wasn't sure what remained. But it felt good, whatever it was. It felt…just *liberating*.

Panting, she repeatedly bumped her forehead against his upper chest. A soothing rhythm. So solid. Comforting, a constant. Something on which she could lean.

Jackie acted before her brain could convince her to stop. She angled her chin high and kissed the rough skin of his throat. She felt him shiver, loosen the bear trap. Circulation tingled down her forearms and hands. Panting still, she fisted his coveralls on either side of his lower back to keep herself against him. More kisses to his throat, his chin and perfect jaw.

When she turned her face to his and saw him looking back at her, she knew why he'd done it. It was there, all over his face, in his dark eyes that had grown red and watery. His bottom lip looked swollen. He didn't seem to mind or to care.

She meant to say "thank you" but knew it just wouldn't convey the depth of her appreciation for what he'd done, the affection she felt for him. Instead, she'd *show* him.

"Kiss me," she whispered, voice too raw to speak aloud.

When he bent over her, abrupt, territorial, Jackie gasped. The heat of his mouth closing on hers triggered painful cramps of anticipation down below.

"Kiss me," she went on as she pulled from his mouth to nibble his chin. "Like you did. Everywhere. Kiss me."

Ty relaxed his unyielding hold to cup her butt and bend her back. To show him she wanted this, that she trusted him and realized—appreciated—what he'd done, she let herself go, let him call the shots. Within seconds he'd reduced both nipples to throbbing points again, just as he'd done with the honey. He licked and bit, sucked and kissed. The faint remnants of honey reached her nose, made her close her eyes and sigh in contentment.

"Ty," she whispered. "What you did... Thank you."

"Shh."

He spent a long time kissing and loving her breasts and her throat, at times gentle, others with primal intensity. She loved it all. Patiently waited for more. Instead of *taking* what she wanted, as she usually did, as the tough Jackie Clark always did, Jacqueline would wait for it. A nice change. All about choices.

"Maybe I should kick things up a notch if you're falling asleep," he remarked before capturing her mouth with his.

Heat. A firestorm of stimuli.

With his mouth that still tasted of honey and man, and with his pitiless hands he claimed her. Arching to give him room to maneuver, Jackie grabbed the console ledge digging into her lower back. Grabbed with both hands and let her head loll backward. Ty took the invitation, the temporary surrender. Took everything she gave him because he must have known a woman like her didn't give often. Not that sort of gift, anyway.

"You have no idea," he growled before covering a nipple with his mouth. Jackie moaned when he sucked hard, tugged then let it slip. "You have *no idea.*"

A long, dry sound made her look as he zipped his coveralls down to his crotch, hurriedly shrugged them off to reveal his hard and muscled body still smelling of soap. Smelling of Terrence Weller.

With lust making his eyes twin shards of obsidian, Ty slipped a hand into her pants, fisted the waistband and belt then yanked her to him, arced her spine in a C and made her feel like an offering. Something that should piss her off but didn't. Choices.

"You've been keeping me on my toes," he growled.

He licked his lips as he let his gaze travel down to her exposed breasts. His fist tightened even more as he hoisted her higher against him by the fistful of pants. His shoulder and biceps bulged with the effort.

"Did you enjoy it, gorgeous? Keeping me on my toes?"

She nodded, licked her lips. God, she *had*.

"Well, now it's my turn."

Jackie gasped when he whirled her around, plastered himself against her, trapped her there while he worked her belt and the closure of her pants with one hand, rolled a nipple with the other. She'd never had a man treat her this way. Never *allowed* one to do this to her. He'd gone from the patient man who'd let her punch him on the snout and knee him in the crotch, to the fierce lover who'd take what he wanted and set her blood to boiling. She loved both.

Cool air greeted her pussy when Ty pulled her pants and panties down around her knees. His muscled thighs pressed against the back of hers.

"Spread your feet," he whispered in her ear.

She was barely able to draw breath. Visions filled her mind's eye. Heat everywhere. Jackie frantically kicked off the flip-flops, pulled a foot out of her pants so she could widen her stance and curl her butt up against him. With a hand both precise and forceful, he followed her natural curve and pressed his palm against her cleft. Juices slicked it.

"Mmm, all that for me?"

"You worked hard for it," she replied half teasing. "It's all yours."

Fingers found her clit, proceeded to rub 'round and 'round, front to back. Heavy then light. Quick then slow.

"I did," he murmured with that voice of his. "But then again, it wasn't really work, was it?" He accentuated the pressure. "You like that?"

"Yes," she gasped. "Don't you stop."

"You're not calling the shots, gorgeous. I am. And now that a couple of things are settled, I think we need more honey."

She actually heard the squirt a second before he licked a long, leisurely pass up her spine. Cramps made her thighs feel as if someone were trying to force them in tight while she struggled to keep them wide. Stars popped around her peripheral vision. Still Ty's fingers worked her. He slipped one into her. Then another long lick up her back.

"Oh God!"

"Believe me," Ty murmured behind her. "He has nothing to do with this."

One finger became two. In and out. Another moan escaped her. Then another, louder. Her clit throbbed, hardened. More juices. More honey. Precursors of release constricted her cleft. After the emotional roller coaster, her senses already fired, it wouldn't take long. Close now. Ty abruptly pulled his hand away. For a split second she arched her butt impotently. Come on.

The clack of skin against skin shocked her. Heat hit right after.

He'd slapped her butt again?! Fever spread from her stinging cheek to her sex. With a ragged cry she came.

"Yeah, that's it," Ty growled as he anchored her by the hips. "Let me hear it!"

She'd never screamed so damn loud. Fingers returned to her clit, rubbed, rubbed, claimed and thrust. Another wave rose.

"Take it," she pushed through her teeth. She couldn't curl her butt any higher so she leaned forward low, spread her legs wider. She'd emotionally given herself to the friend he represented. Now she wanted to do the same physically. To the man, the lover. "Take me...come on...do it."

He did.

The force of his initial penetration lifted her heels off the deck. She cried long and hard. Pleasure ripped through her, pleasure and mind-blowing heat. From her pussy to her anus. From her nipples to her belly. As if she'd been dunked in hot water.

He matched her cries with low grunts. Pulled away then pushed back in. Pounded himself into her as if he wanted to dispel any lingering whispers of her pain and fear and replace them with his attention and skill. Distended her flesh and claimed it with his heat and his strength. Jackie's raw voice broke when the rhythm accentuated. Despite the brutal thrusts, Ty kept his hands against the edge to make them a buffer between her hipbones and the metal console edge. Again showing the kind man inside the rough exterior. Jackie was starting to like that complex man more with each passing second. Maybe more than like.

"Take it!" she urged over and over.

Then as abruptly as he'd taken her, he left her standing there, burning for his touch, for his cock deep in her, feeling him move.

Before she could voice her frustration—and she had an earful for him—Ty grabbed her wrist and yanked her back against him. Just as she thought they were about to fall and hit the deck hard—that'd leave a good mark—he collapsed into his ruined seat, took her with him. She landed sideways, knocked her knee against the armrest.

"Come on," he pushed through his teeth.

Shocked at how long she could last without losing her edge—she'd been so close to coming—she lifted a knee, bit her lip when he took the opportunity to lick his hand and rub her cleft, then sank around him.

Fingers digging deep, he grabbed her hips. "I've been wanting to do this from the get-go, gorgeous." His mouth curled up wickedly. "Been wanting you to *fuck* yourself on me."

Fire spread as she lifted herself off him then sank back down. Slow and measured, nice and methodical. He accompanied her sigh with low groans that swelled his wide chest even more. One hand around his nape, she took him in again, deep and steady.

"Faster," he snapped, bucked up.

A gasp escaped her.

With her thighs burning from the effort, she pulled up almost high enough to separate, but as she stopped there at the apex of slamming back as had been her first instinct, she rolled her hips as she came down, effectively corkscrewed along his shaft. His eyes flared, as did his nostrils.

"Oh you little..."

Jackie did it again. This time she hadn't fully extended her legs when Ty bucked prematurely. Another buck. She stood poised, using his strong neck as an anchor, an armrest for support.

Skin against skin. The wet clack of primal lovemaking. The smells of it too. Musk, honey, sweat. Adrenaline pumped her veins. Stars fizzed at the edge of her vision. She bit down as she slammed back against his muscled thighs, which he'd widened. Her flesh felt sticky with her cum and the honey he'd slathered there.

"Come on," he snarled. His hands became vise grips. "Take me deep."

Both cried out in unison. Jackie could no longer control her movements as Ty wrapped an arm around her, tipped her far back and proceeded to take her deep. Deeper. Hard. Harder.

She abandoned all pretense at control. He could take it all. It was his anyway. Fire licked her pussy. Her clit. Her voice took on a raw quality. His name resounded over and over. And still Ty fucked her with renewed vigor. Voice hoarse, he said things to her, taunted and teased, threatened her with even more pleasure.

The deck hit her on the back. She *humph*-ed loudly. They'd fallen over with him on top. She hadn't even felt the movement.

God, he was heavy. She loved the pressure, the hard body crushing her. It must have been murder on his kneecaps and elbows, but he didn't seem to notice or care as he pushed in, retreated, claimed her again. She used her voice as she would a whip, urging him, taunting him, challenging Terrence Weller to do it, to take her, to take it all. He did. God, he did.

From rhythmic and powerful, his hip work became erratic and wild. One last thrust that rubbed her clit before a veritable firestorm engulfed her. She might have cried out his name. Jackie wasn't sure. Except that as he came, as his cum jetted in burning-hot salvoes and she herself climaxed violently, nothing had ever felt so vivid and vibrant. Like a bright summer day after a long, gray winter. Colors, sounds, smells of him and the feel of his powerful body plastered against her, his hands working their way underneath her head and neck so he could encircle her for a long embrace, literally wrap himself around her. She'd never felt so sheltered. This was the true gift he'd given her. Liberation. The realization she wasn't alone to tackle all of the responsibilities, that if she needed it, she had someone there to help. Ty Weller.

"Gorgeous," he hissed, swallowed hard. "Damn, gorgeous, it's like..." He cursed, gave her a squeeze-grunt combination. "It's like I've been meant to do this all my life. Crazy."

Crazy. She smiled. She probably was. For him. For what they could do together.

After a chuckle, he kissed her head. "When I can fire two neurons together again, I'm pushing you into my shower and getting you all nice and soapy. Mmm."

She closed her eyes, grinned. "'Mmm' is right."

A *whoop* left her after he pulled a hand from under her, squeezed her butt. "We make one helluva team, Clark," he panted, pressed on his busted bottom lip with two fingers. "And who knew you could hit like that! Shit!"

Heat rushed to her face. "I'm sorry, Ty. It was just... It just all came out at once. I didn't mean to."

"I had it coming. Actually, I wanted it. I'm just not the kind of guy who'd let his woman carry all that shit around alone."

"*His* woman?"

"Hell yeah. Even if it was the most dangerous and stupid—in a *good* way, gorgeous, don't look at me like that— bit of flying I've ever seen, you got my ship back and saved me from having to sell my ass as a sex slave to pay for Lydia's schooling. Doesn't get better than this. So you *are* my woman now."

What could she say to that? Face flushed and heart beating madly, she peeled the hand from her butt and kissed the ruined skin of his knuckles. So many scars. She closed her eyes briefly to better feel him still deep in her, nice and warm and slick. "I feel I should thank you again. You're a good man, Terrence Weller. I don't care what anyone says."

Ty chuckled, kissed her sweaty forehead. "Did I tell you, you have the finest ass I've ever seen?"

"Yes, you did."

"Liar. You're such a hussy."

"Thank you."

They shared a quiet laugh as he pulled out. But instead of leaving her, he kissed his way down between her breasts, helped her sit up then gave her a bone-crushing hug.

"I have a proposition for you, Jackie Clark." His sweaty chest and shoulders glistened in temptation. She wasn't the only one getting "all nice and soapy" later on.

"What do you say we pool our resources, your skills, my connections—"

"I have connections too." Old habits die hard. She'd have to learn she didn't need to be the rough and tough courier around Ty. She just needed to be herself. Sometimes hard, sometimes soft.

Ty rolled his eyes. "Would you just give me a moment?"

He retrieved his coveralls, shook them out so he could make a blanket of them then patted the deck. With a grin and a shake of her head, she leaned on her elbow, sighed with contentment when he did the same facing her. From her position, she could see the consoles and the viewscreen across the flight deck, the news was still on. The old rage didn't burn as much as it once did, but still stung. Jackie willed it to subside. She willed herself to accept that she couldn't control everything, that she had someone who'd be there for her. She didn't know for how long and wouldn't ask, but if she knew Ty Weller the way she thought she did, he'd be there for the long run. As stubborn as she was. More.

"You were at the point where we 'pool our resources'," she began.

"Yeah, and I'm not even trying for the sexual innuendo, if you can believe that. Not bad, Weller, not bad." He energetically rubbed his head. "Okay, it's like this—and please don't interrupt me, gorgeous. It's not every day I make this sort of proposition. So. We pool our resources, a sort of co-op, see, then each run gets us, say, forty-sixty depending on who got the call first."

"Fifty-fifty."

"Christ. Fine, fifty-goddamn-fifty. Happy? Where was I? Oh yeah, spanking your ass."

"You already did that." She tried to tame her chuckle, failed.

He pointed to his temple. "Making a list here, that's two spankings for you, Miss Gorgeous. So, what do you say? You in?"

Ty stuck his hand out, his expression a mix of hard competitor and loving man. She raised herself a bit to shake it.

With the angle she could read along the bottom of the screen a banner scrolling in blood red. *Breaking News – deadly virus decimating Livorno outpost – Red Star humanitarian organization is powerless to reach the region due to solar storm...*

Instead of shock and powerlessness, a feeling of intent filled Jackie. Something snapped into place. Everything would be all right. She knew it with the same unshakable certainty that had made her fly her ship directly at a gas giant to retrieve Ty's crippled craft.

"I'm in, Terrence Weller." With a nod, she shook his hand.

"And someday, you're gonna tell me why you flew your old clunker right at a gas giant."

"To get your ship back. It was the right thing to do. My mess to fix."

Ty arched his pierced eyebrow. "See? I don't remember you being like that. You never did anything for free."

"People change. They grow. They start to like someone and things change."

Ty arched his pierced eyebrow. "'Like someone', hmm?"

"Hey, you showed me yours, now I'm showing you mine." She punctuated "yours" and "mine" with a jab of her index finger in his chest. "And what's with the ring?"

"You don't like?"

"I do, makes you look all rebel and wicked."

Big grin. "Ha. Lydia thinks it makes me look too scary. I'll make sure to tell her it's working with the ladies. Or better yet, you tell her."

She hadn't lost the emphasis on the word "you" and recognized an invitation when one was offered to her. "I'd love to meet her. And it's on the way to Livorno."

"Why Livorno?"

Jackie pointed at the news screen.

He craned his neck and looked back. "You want to get involved in that?"

"I think they'll need all the couriers they can get because that storm's keeping the bigger ships from flying. Ours can handle the solar activity. I think we should do it."

Ty shrugged. "Mine can, but yours? I don't know." A punch on the shoulder made him laugh. "Shit, gorgeous, can't a guy make a fucking joke? And the pay must just *suck*."

"Maybe, I'm not sure. Red Star is known to contract couriers all the time to deliver cargo and data to remote regions." She took a long look at him, the man who'd been so intimidating and seductive to her a few years ago and who'd now become someone very important to her. Special. Cherished. "It'd be the right thing to do," she went on. "We should help."

"Why do I get the feeling we're about to put our asses on the line to help the widows and orphans and puppies everywhere? For fuck's sake, we just got here. My ship isn't even in flying condition yet."

"I'll help." The way he'd helped her get rid of the rage and the fear. "Plus, I owe you."

His expression turned serious. "Don't you say that. You don't owe me anything. Clear? If I'm hanging around it's because I like it, not because I'm waiting for you to pay up."

Affection growing by the minute, Jackie nodded, cleared her throat to give herself some countenance.

He grimaced. "You gonna cry?"

She loved the way he could change from affectionate to dominating, from gentle to rough, sensitive to playful.

So she followed him there. Giving him the infamous lopsided grin, she fanned the air. "Danger and adrenaline," she yawned theatrically, "scary stuff, I know."

"You calling me a chicken?"

"Me? Never."

A sparkle appeared in his eyes. Then in the way she'd come to love, his expression again did a three-sixty and turned from genial to feral. He reeled her in, put his mouth directly by her ear. "So tell me, gorgeous, any guy out there who thinks you belong to him? Anyone who needs his kneecaps looked at?"

"Just one, but he's a large, irritable man with no hair and a big mouth."

He pulled back, huffed a curse. "Hey, I *shave* it."

Jackie chuckled. Her life hadn't been boring so far. She had an idea it'd become even less so with a man like Terrence Weller on her radar screen.

"Argh, Christ, I guess we should get some sleep before we fix our ships and play saviors to the thankful-but-penniless masses."

"Sleep?" she replied, knowing her grin would do its job.

"Never mind."

SIN IN JEANS
Ciana Stone

ဆ

Dedication

ଯ

For Chase. Surely no woman has been more blessed than I to have a friend like you.

Prologue

ॐ

Myth, magic or legend? There have been Hussies since before time was measured in days and minutes. Women who fought bravely alongside their mates with sword and axe, warriors whose courage changed the world around them. Led by the first Hussy, Danu, these fierce fighters discovered their inner strengths, summoned reserves they didn't know they possessed and passed into the fabric of legend with their daring exploits.

Since that time, myths have been spun around the Hussy Warriors—tales told by firelight, whispered from mother to daughter—eventually to take their place amongst the mystical fables that shape our souls.

But the essence of a Hussy remains strong in the hearts of so many women. Heroines who don't realize that within them lies the power to make a difference, to effect change, to use their passion every bit as skillfully as Danu wielded her sword so long ago. Warriors in different times and different places, who love as deeply and desire as desperately as any woman ever has, seldom knowing that their desire will impact not just one man, but so much more.

Therein lies the magic of a Hussy. To right a wrong, turn a frown to a smile—to positively change those around her. To love a man with every fiber of her body, to learn from that love and to grow stronger because of it.

Whether in the past, the future, or the here-and-now, there are Hussies around each corner. They may not even be aware of their Hussy destiny. But one thing is certain—when passion knocks on their door, lives will change for the better.

And when it comes to their one special hero? Well, he's in for the ride of his life.

Which leaves one unanswered question...are *you* a Hussy?

Chapter One

ℬ

Dale unhooked the trailer, locked it and left it in the back of the parking lot as the hotel manager had directed. She was road weary and hungry. The drive from North Carolina had taken longer than she'd anticipated thanks to road construction. Now all she wanted was a shower, something to eat and a good night's sleep.

She grabbed her overnight bag from the truck and headed for the lobby to ask if they had a restaurant. Maybe she'd just call in for room service instead of trying to find a good place to eat.

Just as she neared the door, she noticed two things. One, that a stunningly beautiful woman in an elegant dress and heels, with platinum-blonde hair was crossing the parking lot ahead of her. And two, that the car coming around the corner wasn't slowing at all.

"Hey!" she yelled and broke into a run. "Hey, lady!"

The woman didn't appear to hear her and the car was still coming. Dale stepped it up a notch and made a dive for the woman. Two seconds after she'd wrapped her arm around the woman and made a mighty leap for safety, the car sped by.

Dale and the woman both teetered unsteadily for a few moments, Dale trying to balance her overnight bag and hang onto the woman, whose high-heeled shoes didn't really lend themselves for quick maneuvers.

When they finally steadied, Dale released the woman.

"Oh my," the woman exclaimed softly. "My dear, thank you."

"Sure," Dale replied with a smile.

"You saved my life."

"Oh I doubt it would have killed you," Dale said, feeling the compliment was a bit exaggerated. "Banged you up some, but you'd have survived."

"Still, you risked yourself to help a stranger. That's rare in today's world."

"Not where I come from."

"Then you must hail from a wonderful place, my dear."

"Yeah, it's nice. Pretty land and good folks. Can't ask for much more than that."

"I fear most people have a different view today. You're a refreshing change. And I do thank you. If not for saving my life, then for saving me from what would have most certainly been a painful experience."

"You're welcome. Have a good one." Dale started for the hotel door, but the woman reached out and put her hand on Dale's arm.

"Wait, please. I feel I should do something to thank you."

"You just did."

"I mean something...demonstrative."

"That's not necessary. Really. But thanks for the offer."

"No, please. I insist."

Dale didn't want to be compensated for doing what any decent person would have done. She just wanted to take a shower, eat and get some sleep. But she couldn't be rude to someone who was trying so hard to show their gratitude.

"I really don't want anything, ma'am."

"Well, perhaps this will be something that will prove valuable to you at a later date." She rummaged in her small purse for a moment and pulled out a smooth gray stone. It covered the palm of her hand, rather flat and not quite circular.

"A rock?" Dale asked when the woman handed it to her.

"From my homeland."

"Oh, well thank you, but if you carry this around then it must be important to you, so it wouldn't be right for me to take it."

"I insist," the woman said. "I suspect it may prove beneficial."

Dale couldn't imagine how a rock would benefit her, but she wasn't going to argue the point. It obviously meant something to the woman so to dishonor that value would be the worst kind of insult. And like her grandma had taught her, anything a person put that much value on had to be a powerful object.

"Thank you," she said and tucked it into the pocket of her jeans. "I'll keep it with me right here and not let anything happen to it."

"May it assist you in what will most certainly be the most pivotal time of your life, Dale," the woman replied and turned away, leaving Dale staring at her back with her mouth hanging open.

How did that woman know her name?

"Hey!" she called out, but the woman did not stop or turn back. Dale stared at her as she entered the hotel, then shrugged and hitched her bag up on her shoulder and followed.

There was no sign of the woman in the lobby. Figuring she'd already headed for her room, Dale checked to see if there was a restaurant in house. The clerk told her it was currently closed for renovations but would be happy to suggest restaurants if Dale would tell him what type of food she was interested in.

Feeling very unsophisticated, she asked for the closest place that served real burgers and beer. The clerk smiled and wrote down the name and directions for her. Taking a look at the card, she headed for her room. Thoughts of a thick, juicy burger and a tall cold beer had her stomach rumbling.

* * * * *

Tyler laughed at the old joke more out of politeness than humor. Shorty Smith was a good old boy, but left a lot to be desired when it came to getting a punch line right.

"So whatever happened to that little filly you was courting over to St. Cloud?" Shorty asked after downing the rest of his beer.

Tyler grimaced. His short-lived romance with Rebecca Hastings was not something he wanted to talk about. In hindsight he wondered why he'd ever gotten hooked up with the woman. Sure she was easy on the eyes, but talk about high maintenance. Her idea of a good time and his were about as far apart as Venus and Jupiter.

He was happy having a burger at Roscoe's, a couple of brews and settling down in front of the television to watch some PBR. Or going kayaking, or riding, or hell, working. But dressing up in a suit and tie and spending two hundred dollars on a meal that should have cost nine-ninety-five, or dropping a hundred bucks on drinks at a ritzy bar was not his idea of a good time. Nor was shopping. Good lord, did that woman like to shop. With other people's money.

Fact was Tyler was starting to think that God hadn't made a woman that was right for him. Hell, he had three ex-wives and a dozen ex-girlfriends to support the theory. Maybe his father was right and some men just weren't cut out for hearth and home. He didn't want to think he'd spend his life alone, but it sure was starting to look that way.

"Let's not go there," he said to Shorty.

"Damn, Ty, you sure go through the women," Shorty said with a laugh, then his eyebrows rose sky high. "Well, now, would you look at that?"

Tyler turned to look behind him and at that moment Shorty stumbled against him, sending Tyler bumping up into the object of their attention.

Dale cursed as the beer she was lifting suddenly sloshed over the rim of the mug, down the front of her t-shirt and onto her jeans. Her head whipped around, eyes narrowed and ready to give whoever had jostled her a tongue-lashing to beat the band.

And went brain dead. Completely mute without the ability to utter a word.

"'Scuse me," the tall man with the worn Stetson, faded denim shirt rolled up to expose strong forearms and eyes the color of a Carolina sky said with a smile. "Ol' Shorty back there's a little deep in the cups and fell against me."

"Oh well...that's okay. Accidents happen," she said, finding her tongue.

The man signaled to the bartender. "A draft, Jimmy? And one here for the lady."

"That's not necessary," Dale protested. "Really."

"Yeah, it is," the man replied and angled to face her, propping one elbow on the bar. "Haven't seen you here before. You new?"

"Just passing through. Here to see a man about a horse."

"That almost sounds like the truth. 'Cept there's no horses here."

"A fella at the Inn said it was a good place to have a beer, a burger and not be in the middle of the mouse crowd, whatever that is."

Another laugh from the man had something warm curling in her belly. Damn if he wasn't sexy. And not trying to be, she'd guess. The smell of soap said he'd showered, but the five o'clock shadow said he hadn't taken time to shave. Which meant he either thought the rough look was more appealing or he didn't much care.

She suspected the latter. The shirt had seen better days, the jeans were worn and faded and those sure weren't dress boots on his feet. He wasn't dressed to impress, which meant it

111

was more likely that he was just relaxing with friends, not on the prowl.

"Mouse crowd means tourists," he explained and thanked the bartender for the beers. "We are in Mickey's backyard, you know."

"I guess so. Well, if the burgers here are any good, then the fella did me a good turn."

"Burgers are real good," he said and looked around. "You here alone or is there a Mr. Here to See a Man About a Horse getting ready to bust my chops for hittin' on his woman?"

"Is that what you're doing?"

"Is there a fist in my face coming if I say yes?"

"No danger of that."

He grinned and lifted his mug to his mouth, eyeing her over the rim before he drank. "Then I reckon it is. How'm I doin'?"

"Not bad." She gave him a teasing smile. "But you could try a little harder."

Throwing back his head, he laughed. A low, sexy laugh that sent a delightful little shiver straight down all the way to her toes. "Well, honey, I think I can muster up a little more effort. What say you and me grab that empty booth, have another beer and order up some burgers?"

"Hey now, you're starting to speak my language. Seducing me with grilled meat and beer. Lead the way, cowboy."

"This way, ma'am," he said and led the way.

It was pure pleasure watching the man walk. He had that low-center-of-gravity, loose-hipped walk that only one breed of man possessed. A man who spent time in the saddle.

Strong long legs led to a firm tight butt and on up a lean back that flared into very nice broad shoulders. There didn't appear to be any spare meat on him. He was lean and long, just the kind of man who switched all the neurons in her brain from reason to lust. Just the kind of man that had her all too willing to say I do.

Dale had to remind herself that she wasn't there looking for love. In fact, the L word had been stricken from her vocabulary for good. All love had ever gotten her was trouble.

But lust? Now that was a horse she could ride.

He slid into one side of the empty booth and she took the opposite side. "So I'm assuming you're not a stranger here," she commented, noticing the greetings he got from people as they'd made their way to the table, and the narrowing of more than one set of female eyes.

"Guess you could say I'm a regular."

"From around these parts?"

"A ways south."

She nodded and took a drink of her beer. Just then a waitress appeared at the table. "Hey, handsome. Haven't seen you all week. Where you been hiding?"

"Same as always, sugar. Can we get a couple of burgers with fries and two more drafts?"

"Sure thing," the waitress said with a grin. "Usual fixins'?"

"Yes, ma'am."

"How 'bout you, honey?" the woman asked Dale.

"Just bring me whatever he's having," Dale replied, earning raised eyebrows from the waitress.

"You want a double burger with the works? Honey, those things are big enough to choke a horse."

"Sounds good," Dale replied with a smile.

"Well, all righty then." The waitress popped her pad in the pocket of her apron and sashayed away.

"So," Tyler said. "You have a name, pretty lady?"

"Well, yes I do," Dale replied with just as much flirtation as had been in the question. "How 'bout you, cowboy? On second thought, no don't tell me. Rusty. Colby. Chance. Chase. Rowdy. Slim. Am I getting warm?"

"How 'bout plain ol' Ty?" he asked.

"That'll do."

"And you'd be?"

"Plain ol' Dale."

"Nothing plain about you, sugar. So, would that be Mrs., Ms. or Miss?"

"Anything but Mrs."

"Sounds like you don't think much of marriage."

Tyler had a hard time believing that a woman with Dale's looks hadn't had at least one brush with marriage. She was a real honey. Long dark hair that was beginning to see a few streaks of gray that she obviously felt no need to hide, and a face that was devoid of makeup but possessed of a pair of the most beautiful golden brown eyes he'd ever seen in his life that were rimmed with lashes so thick it's a wonder some woman hadn't killed her in envy.

Her body was the kind that made his mouth water. Small in stature, but with nice full round breasts, slim hips and strong legs. She looked like the kind of woman who wasn't afraid to get dirty or work hard and was sexier than all the painted dolls currently populating the bar.

"Actually I think highly of it. It just doesn't fit me very well. At least not according to my ex-husbands."

"Was that a plural?"

"'Fraid so."

"So we talking two, three or thirty-three?"

"Two. How 'bout you? Is there a Mrs. Ty out there?"

"There's a few of them. No current ones though. Seems that marriage doesn't like me all that much either. At least not for the long run. My mama swears that it'll be a long row to hoe to find a woman who can put up with me for the long haul."

"And why's that?"

"I guess I tend to be a little set in my ways."

"Oh yeah? Like?"

"Oh you know, normal stuff like I want my woman at home at night with me, not out gallivanting with her girlfriends. And I don't particularly like the idea of my wife taking a cruise to the Bahamas and leaving me at home because she needs her own space."

"Well, that doesn't sound too unreasonable."

"Tell my ex-wives that."

Dale laughed. It didn't appear that Ty had much to hide. Not about his failed marriages or the fact that he had certain old-fashioned expectations. She liked that. Honesty made life a lot simpler.

She looked around the bar then back at Ty. Their eyes met and suddenly the room seemed a whole lot smaller. And hotter. Or maybe it was just her. She wasn't a stranger to lust, and recognized the look in his eyes. Aside from the jesting and teasing way they'd couched the conversation, they'd both been feeling each other out, getting the lay of the land. And now they both knew there was nothing stopping them if they wanted to take the chance encounter to another level.

Question was, did she? Dale had never been much on one-night stands. Hell, she didn't even rank in that category. Her one one-night stand had ended up with her and the object of her lust standing in front of a Vegas preacher at three in the morning getting hitched.

It'd taken her ninety minutes to get married and nineteen months to get out of it. Since the day she got rid of mistake number two, she'd vowed not to let herself fall victim to making the same kind of mistake.

But Ty didn't appear to be the kind of man who'd rush off to a preacher on a whim. Behind the sexy smile and good ol' boy charm lurked sharpness and a wariness that was hard to hide. Dale's grandma had always told her she had a knack for reading folks if she'd just trust her instinct. And right now, her instinct was telling her that a one-night stand with Ty might just be quite satisfying. But falling in love? She didn't think there was much danger in that. They were both losers in the marriage department and that made a person leery about jumping in with their emotions too fast.

Lust, however, wasn't necessarily a kissing cousin to love. And lust was something she had in plenty at the moment. It was even muffling her hunger for that burger. And dampening her hunger took something powerful.

Ty could almost see the wheels turning in Dale's head. She was skittish when it came to men. Probably because she'd been burned twice. And maybe because while she could talk the talk, she really didn't walk the walk too well. Teasing and flirting seemed to come natural. But letting things progress beyond a flirtation with a stranger over a beer and burgers was something he wasn't sure she was prepared for.

However, he wanted to find out. And that was curious. She was a looker. No doubt of that. But he'd had his share of pretty women, and the old saying about beauty only being skin deep was truer than folks realized. So it couldn't be just her looks that got to him. Hell, if it was just looks he was after, he could skedaddle over to Rebecca's and have a romp. Not a real good one, but it'd be enough to take the edge off that fever that was starting to make the crotch of his jeans feel too tight and his fingers itch to tangle in Dale's hair.

But he didn't want Rebecca. He wanted the woman sitting across from him. The woman he knew nothing about except the fact that the way she looked at him made him want to be out of the bar and between her legs.

And what did he have to lose by testing the water to see if she'd swim?

"So, Dale, what kinda plans you got for later on?"

"Bed," she said without hesitation, her eyes glued to him.

"Alone?"

"If I was smart, yes."

"And are you smart?"

"I'd like to think so, but the truth is, right now my brain isn't really in control, Ty."

"That so?"

"Yeah."

"So what we gonna do about that, baby?"

"I don't know."

"Then who does?"

She shrugged and propped her forearms on the table to lean a little toward him. "Look, we're strangers and probably won't ever see each other after tonight, but still, I don't believe in lying, so I'm gonna give it to you straight. You're walking sin, Ty, and that's no bull. Long and lean and muscles in all the right places. Right now I'd give up that burger even though I'm hungry enough to eat the south end of a northbound cow and drag you out to my truck and have at it.

"But," she paused, "I am smart enough to know that you and I know nothing about each other and it's damn stupid for a woman to trust a stranger, so I'm a little hesitant to act on my wants."

He hadn't expected truth and was a little taken aback. She out and out admitted that she wanted him but didn't trust him as far as she could toss him.

"You do shoot straight, don't you, Dale?"

"Is there any other way?"

"No. And I admire that. It's smart. We are strangers and for all you know I could be the kind of man who'd sooner beat the shit out of a woman as love her."

"But?" she asked with a sly smile that had his pulse hammering.

"But...well, I guess you could take my phone and poll all the ladies in my address book for references."

"And just what would they have to say, Ty?"

"That if you're looking for happily ever after, don't look at me. I don't like to shop. I'm not gonna spend two hundred dollars on dinner and if you think for one red-hot second that I'm gonna take ballroom dance classes then you need to have your head checked."

"Hmmm, well, since I'm not looking for any of those things, what could they tell me about what kind of lover you are, Ty?"

"That would depend on who you talk to."

"Which means?"

He leaned forward, taking one of her hands in his. "That when it comes to loving a woman, I do my damn best to give her what she wants and how she wants it."

"Well now, that's high praise," she said in a slightly huskier tone.

"Just fact."

"So why don't we get those burgers to go, cowboy?" The moment the words were out of her mouth, Dale was sure she could have cut her tongue out. Damn, was her brain on total hiatus?

His eyes registered surprise but his lips curved in a smile. A smile that promised something she wasn't sure she was ready for. But what was done was done, and she'd never welshed on a deal in her life. On anything.

"Well, now, why don't we just do that?" He looked across the bar and yelled, "Hey, Shirley! Wrap that up to go, honey!"

"Let me take care of the bill," he said and stood.

"I'll pay for my own," she said, getting to her feet.

"I got it covered. Meet me outside."

With that he strode across the bar. Dale blew out her breath and headed for the door. Outside the air was muggy and thick. Within seconds her hair was sticking to the back of her neck. She leaned against the rail that encompassed the small walkway circling the building and lifted her hair up off her neck.

When the door opened and Ty walked out, not even shaving her head would have cooled her off. Carrying a brown paper bag in his hand, he walked over and stopped in front of her.

"Before we go any further, we need to know," he said and reached one hand behind her neck to pull her to her feet and to him.

His lips parted as soon as they made contact with hers. He tasted of beer and whatever was unique to him and it was a heady combination. So heady that she forgot she was standing in public. Forgot she didn't know him from Adam's house cat. And gave herself to this kiss.

He was neither shy nor hesitant but neither was he rough. His tongue explored as his mouth slanted for better contact. He was slow and deliberate and thoroughly intoxicating. She leaned in against him and felt his hand holding the bag move around and press against the small of her back.

Which put her in direct contact with empirical evidence that the kiss was affecting him pretty much in the same way it was her because his erection pressed against her belly in an all-too-tempting manner.

Dale didn't care that her arms crept up to wind around his neck. Or that the sound in her throat was one of hunger and need. Or that they just might be making a spectacle of

119

themselves. All she cared about was the feel of him against her and their joined lips.

The kiss lingered long enough that it would qualify for making out in public, something that became evident when a voice came from behind Ty, "Good lord and a quarter, Ty. Get a room!"

Ty broke the kiss to look over his shoulder. "Sounds like a good idea, Shorty. Drive safe."

"Well?" Dale asked when he turned his attention back to her. "Do we know?"

"Oh yeah, we know. You want to come to my place?"

"Why don't you come to mine?"

"Where is that?"

"The Inn down on Vine."

"Where's your car?"

"My truck's over there," she pointed.

"I'm right in front of you," he replied and took her hand. "Come on. I'll follow you."

Chapter Two

Dale parked her truck and just sat there, staring through the windshield. What the hell was she doing? The drive to the Inn had given her time to cool down a little from the kiss. Time to ask herself if she was making a huge mistake.

Her head said yes. Her libido said "shut the hell up" to her head. And she was somewhere in the middle, watching the battle and wondering which side to cheer for. The answer came in the form of Ty, who parked his truck across the lot from her. Watching him walk across the parking lot toward her got her blood to singing again. Fast.

The victor of the battle emerged. Libido triumphed over brains.

She climbed out of the truck and met him before he reached her. "I'm in 107," she said.

He fell in step with her and she couldn't help wondering if he was having misgivings. Neither of them spoke and it was a little uncomfortable. Was he as nervous as she was?

That question was answered when she unlocked the door and walked in. He followed and before the door closed behind him, took her by the arm, turned her to him and claimed a kiss that had her heart racing and her pants feeling decidedly damp in the crotch.

"God almighty, you're good at that," she breathed against his lips when he waltzed her backward into the room and closer to the bed.

"You ain't seen nothing yet," he promised and tossed his hat aside as he pushed her down onto the bed.

Holy smokes, did he feel good when he stretched out on the length of her, his erection pressed into her belly and his lips devouring hers. Not until that moment did she realize how much she'd longed for something like this, needed it. Realization brought a sense of liberation with it and she returned the kiss with hunger that was as raw and intense as what was given.

Their bodies strained in to one another, hands roaming, touching and squeezing and all the while tongues and lips hungrily feasted.

Ty pulled back from the kiss and sat back on his heels. His hands started at her waist and moved slowly up her sides, lifting her arms as his hands moved up the inside of her elbows to her wrists, his body sinking slowing forward on hers until his hands imprisoned hers above her head.

Her lips parted eagerly when he traced his tongue over them. She sucked his tongue into her mouth, pressing her heels into the bed to lift her pelvis up and grind against that gloriously hard shaft straining at his jeans.

"Hmmm," he murmured, rocking back slowly and letting his hands retrace their way down her arms to the side of her breasts. "Stay just like that, honey. Now don't move."

Dale wasn't much on taking orders, but this one seemed enticing enough to follow. His hands moved over her breasts slowly, fingers circling the hard buttons of her nipples through the fabric of her shirt. When he grabbed the neckline of her t-shirt and ripped it right down the middle she gasped, then smiled.

"Well hello, my beauties," he said in a low, rough voice when her breasts spilled free.

The next gasp that came from her was not one of surprise but a sharp stab of pleasure at his hands gathering her breasts to lift and push them together, all the while tracking over her nipples with his thumbs.

A stampede of sensation radiated out from her nipples and raced quickly down the length of her body, taking root in her sex. Damn, his touch was like electricity, making her nerves sizzle. She started to reach for him, hungry for more of his taste, but he stopped her with a look and a soft whisper.

"Uh-uh, put your hands back where they were, honey. Over your head. Reach up and run your hands under that headboard and hang on."

In typical Dale fashion, her first reaction was to argue. Acting the role of a submissive wasn't her style. She'd meet a man on equal footing and give as good as she got, but submitting was something she'd never acquired a taste for.

"Do it." His voice sent a shiver running down her spine. It was a tone she knew well. The tone of command. Whether it was used on an animal or a person, the inflection was the same, as was the intent. *You're going to do this my way.*

"Do it, honey." His voice was low and rough. "I'll give you what you need."

"You think you know what I need, Ty?"

Cool air whispered over her breasts as his hands released them. Disappointed, she wished she'd given in. His touch was delicious and she wanted more. A split second later disappointment was overpowered by pure heat as he pinched her nipples, rolling them between his thumbs and index fingers. He applied just the right amount of pressure. Enough to make it verge on pain without ever crossing that threshold.

"Christ on a crutch!" She moaned and worked her hands up to the headboard to hang on.

"That's it, baby," he whispered as he lowered his head to flick his tongue over one tight nipple. "And hey, before you ask. I get tested regularly and I'm clean. Got the paperwork to prove it. But if you'd prefer to use protection..."

"Hmmm." She arched up into the sensation. "No need. I'm clean too. Certificate back home in my desk drawer though. Not real inclined to go home to get it."

"No need," he growled against her skin. "I trust you."

When he sucked her nipple into his mouth, the sensation made her cry out. She wanted to dig her fingers into his flesh, tangle her hands in his thick hair and press his face more firmly against her breast. Claw, scratch, something. She just couldn't lie there passive and do nothing. It was too much.

She fisted one hand in his hair, pulling him more firmly against her breast. Sliding her free hand between their bodies, she worked at the button of his jeans.

Ty sat back, smiling at her. "You in a hurry, honey?"

"Take them off. I want to feel you, Ty. Taste you."

"Good manners demand that I let a lady go first," he said as he moved off her.

"Good manners," she said with a snort. "Fine, but you're coming out of those jeans, stud."

She sat and swung her legs over the edge of the bed, leaning down to peel off her boots and socks.

When she stood to peel off her jeans, she looked back over her shoulder at him. He was lying on the bed, propped on one elbow, watching with a sexy smile.

"Don't mind me. Just enjoying the show."

She shot him a smile, turned her back to him and slowly lowered her jeans, baring her ass then her legs as she stepped out of them and turned to face him.

"So country gals favor cotton, eh?"

"All natural fiber," she remarked and slid the thin straps of her thong down over her hips.

Dale watched Ty's eyes move over her. She could almost feel his gaze on her skin, the look on his face making her hotter and wetter. She let her hand move over her belly and down to cup her wet sex. "Your turn, cowboy. Let's see what you got."

Ty smiled and got off the bed. Toeing off his boots, he divested himself of his socks and then unfastened his belt and jeans. Dale climbed onto the bed, her eyes glued to him.

Ty left his jeans unbuttoned and unzipped while he took off his shirt. Great glory, was he fine. The firm swell of his chest was dusted with fine, dark hair that trailed down the center of his firm abdomen to thicken south of his navel and disappear into his jeans.

Dale liked a man with some hair on his body. She particularly liked Ty's body. Lean, strong lines and tanned skin spoke of a man accustomed to work. Not a fellow who got his muscles from pumping iron in a gym, but muscles gained from long hours of hard work that would have most bodybuilders whining and begging for mercy before the day's end.

Ty worked his jeans down over his hips and she felt like jumping up and giving a big rebel yell. He was long and thick, standing at attention.

"Come here." She sat up and grabbed him by the hips as he stepped over to her. One hand wrapped around the base of his shaft as the other worked behind him to grab his ass and pull him closer.

Her tongue circled the swollen head then laved down the length of him. She felt his hands tangle in her hair as she took him in her mouth. Saints above, he was fine. She gave herself over to the taste and feel of him. It wasn't until he gave a slight groan and pulled on her hair that she stopped and looked up at him.

Ty leaned over, his lips locking with hers in a kiss that had her toes curling. He pushed her back on the bed, his long, lean body hot and hard against her. Supporting himself on one elbow, he abandoned her lips to travel down her neck in soft kisses and sharp little bites. And all the while, his hand worked slowly down her body.

When he reached her sex, his hand cupped her. She pressed against his hand, eager for his touch. His fingers moved in her wet folds, spreading her lips to stroke and probe.

She didn't even try to stop the moan of longing that came from deep inside her. At the sound he gave her a wolfish smile and staked a claim on her lips. His fingers moved inside her, deep and slow strokes that had her panting against his mouth and rocking against the movement of his fingers.

"God that feels good," she groaned. "More. More, Ty. More."

"I'm gonna give you more, honey," he whispered against her lips, then sucked her bottom lip into his mouth and bit lightly on it before moving to nip at her chin and work his way down her neck.

"Gonna give you pleasure every way I can think of. And I won't stop until I've had my fill and you're too sore to take any more."

"Talk's cheap," she breathed throatily. "I'm a show-me kinda gal."

Ty's hand tangled in her hair, pulling her head back. He looked down into her eyes and she saw a promise there that had her eager for all he had to give. "Yes," she moaned as his fingers stroked her closer to orgasm.

His headed lowered, mouth closing on her breast. The light bite he gave to her nipple had her crying out. Not in pain, but hunger. He growled against her, not easing up. She worked her hands down his body, circling his shaft. "I want you," she moaned, squeezing him.

"And you're gonna get me, honey," he said against her skin then raised his head to smile at her. "But first..."

He sat back, took hold of her legs and forced them into a bent position, spreading them wide. Her hands worked into fists, clutching at the bedcovers as he licked her wet folds. He spread her legs more, sucking her labia into his mouth, and then slowly moved his tongue up her length to suck on her clit.

126

She moaned when his tongue worked down and plunged inside her. A gasp followed when his tongue stroked inside her, sending a spark of electric sensation tearing through her.

Her hands moved to her inner thighs, pressing them out and down, fingers digging into her own skin as the intensity increased. "That's it, baby," he crooned against her and released her legs to use his fingers to spread her wide, exposing her clit.

Her fingers dug deeper into her flesh when his tongue flicked over her clit, teasing and circling it. She was panting by the time he captured it in his mouth, his tongue tracing over the hard nub.

She trembled, spreading her legs wider, wanting more yet fighting to stem the wave that threatened to wash her out into that sea of release.

Ty pressed two fingers inside her, his strokes slow and deep as he continued the sublime assault on her clit. It was too much. She couldn't hold back.

"Ah god...Ty," she moaned. He went slow, pushing deeper until the length of him was hilted inside her.

He pressed two fingers into her pussy, stroking deep as he continued to suck on her clit. It was more than she could withstand. With a great shudder she exploded. Before the wave had crested, he pulled her forward, pressing the head of his cock at the entrance of her sex.

The wave intensified, leaving her mindless to everything but the sensations. She moaned as the head of his cock penetrated, stretching her wide. He pushed slowly, deeper and deeper inside, until his full length was embedded inside her.

Dale's body strained to accommodate him. She felt stretched to her limits, clenching on the hardness that filled her and all the while imprisoned by an orgasm that had her panting and moaning, her hands gripping his shoulders like claws, digging in and holding fast.

He took his time, stroking slow and stretching the pleasure out so that every time it seemed the intensity would abate, his pace would increase. Hard and deep he rode her, bringing her back to a fevered pitch of sensation so intense all she could do was surrender to its power.

When his movements began to slow, she sucked in a breath and panted at him. "More. Now. Please."

"I want to see you play with yourself. Play with that sweet little clit, honey." He sat back on his heels, pulling her forward so that she was bowed, her hips elevated by his thighs.

She had no problem complying. Securing her position by digging her heels into the bed on either side of him had her pelvis rocking forward, her legs spreading. Her hands moved between her legs, fingers spreading her sex to expose her clit. She saw his eyes tracking her movements.

She ran one finger, then two over that hard bud of flesh, feeling the resulting spark that made her sex clench on him. He gripped her hips, measuring his pace with her. Slow at first, his thrusts increased speed and depth as her body started to tense with the onset of climax.

She felt the vibration begin and at that moment he drove deep inside her. She screamed his name in pleasure and tightened her legs around his waist to pull him down on her.

The slap of flesh on flesh was a percussion beat to the harmony of their fast breaths and her throaty groans. Faster and harder he rode her, his arms bearing his weight so that his chest only brushed her, the rasp of hair against her nipples creating a burn that only added to the sensation that rioted through her.

"Ah, honey," he groaned as she started to contract on him. "You're gonna—"

"Come with me," she panted, milking him in strong contractions. She felt him let go, felt him pulse in time with her contractions and she crested, letting herself freefall into sensation.

When at last the wave had passed, he lowered himself down, rolling over with his arms locked around her so that she lay against his side. With her head on his chest, she closed her eyes, listing to the rapid pound of his heart and feeling her own breath trying to stabilize.

For a long time he held her then drew back and looked into her eyes.

"What?" she asked.

"Just curious. Are you disappointed?"

Dale chuckled and kissed his chest. "Only if you tell me you're done in."

"Not by a long shot."

She raised one eyebrow, feeling her sex clench in excited anticipation. "You think you're ready for round two, cowboy?"

"That depends."

"On?"

"On whether you can handle it."

She laughed and pushed up into a sitting position, lifting her hair up on top of her head. "I'm ready and willing to try. But first, I really need some water. I've got cotton mouth from hell."

"Probably some over there." He gestured toward the small bar in the sitting area with a mini refrigerator and coffeemaker.

She got up and went to the bar. Sure enough there were bottles of cold water in the little refrigerator. "Want one?" she asked.

"Yeah, that'd be good."

She opened one bottle and chugged down half of it as she carried the other across the room. Her eyes fell on the clock beside the bed and she cursed.

"Shit on a stick!"

"What's wrong?" he asked and accepted the water she handed him.

"I'm sorry but I really do need to make a call. Damn, I hate to call this late but..."

"Calling home?"

"No. Calling a man about a horse. I told you I'm here—"

"To see a man about a horse. Yeah. I thought you were joking."

"Not hardly. Do you mind? It'll only take a minute."

"I think I can wait that long."

"Thanks."

She went through the clothes lying scattered on the floor and found her jeans. Her phone was still clipped to the belt.

Sitting down on the bed, she scrolled through the numbers, located the one she needed and placed the call.

Suddenly something buzzed on the floor. Then again.

"Damn!" Ty rolled off the bed and hunted around on the floor. Dale watched as she waited for an answer. When he stood up with a phone in his hand that was ringing, her eyes went wide and a feeling of dread hit her stomach like a lead balloon.

"Answer it," she said.

He gave her a curious look and opened the phone. "Yeah?"

"Hey," she said.

Ty's eyes rounded and his mouth fell open.

"T.D. Austin?" Dale spoke into the phone but her eyes were glued to him.

"Yeah."

"This is R.D. Evans. I'm calling about that Cracker horse I'm supposed to pick up in the morning."

"Fuck me!" Ty said with a laugh, closed the phone and tossed it aside. "This is too good."

"Good?" Dale lay her phone on the nightstand and fell back on the bed with her hands over her face. "Good? What's good about it?"

"Well, at least we know who we're doing business with. Kind of." He lay down beside her on the bed, his hands drifting over her skin.

"R. D. Evans? What does the R stand for?"

She grimaced and sat up to chug down more water. "Roberta."

He grinned up at her. "And you go by Dale."

"Yeah, Dale."

"Dale. Dale Evans."

He tried not to grin or laugh, but at the smile that broke out on her face he let it go. "Dale Evans? As in Roy and Dale?"

She shook her head, laughing with him. "I know, it's horrible. What can I say? My parents were sadists."

"Ah now, it isn't that bad."

"Easy for you to say. You don't come from a family with names like Robert David Jr., Robert Daniel, Robert Drew, Roberta Diane, Roberta Denise and then, of course, me. Roberta Dale."

Tyler grinned at the expression on her face. "Well, your mama and daddy sure had a thing for the name Robert, now didn't they?"

"Oh yeah. But enough of my sad family woes. Tell me about this horse, Mr. T. D. Austin."

"Ty."

"Come on, Ty. Tell me about Belle."

131

Tyler leaned back, propping his hands behind his head, quite comfortable lying there naked discussing horses with her. Their eyes met and sure as he was alive and breathing, the look she gave him had his toes ready to curl and things south of the belt standing up to salute.

"First, let me ask you something, Dale. Why a Cracker horse?"

She lay on her side beside him, taking him in her hand and stroking him gently as she answered. "They're smart, have a good, natural herding instinct and the claim is that they have unusual endurance and strength," she said then added, "And I already own a stallion and want to breed him. When I read about Belle and saw her picture I knew she was the right mare."

"You want to breed them? I thought the Evanses were into bull genetics?"

"We are. See, it's like this. My mother died when I was seventeen. When Dad died a few years ago, he split things up between the kids. I got the horses and part of the cattle and the bulls. My brothers got the rest of the stock and my sisters traded their parts for cash since they never wanted to have anything to do with it anyway."

"And you want to breed Crackers."

"I want to try my hand at it. I don't like seeing something fade away like a good breed of horse. The way things are now, folks like us are already a minority. Most people don't know their ass from a hole in the ground when it comes to farming and ranching and we're getting shoved out by developers in every state. If we don't work to keep our lifestyles and our breeds alive, we're all going the way of the dinosaur. And I don't like that idea."

"Amen, sister. I'm just surprised that you've chosen the Cracker. But I agree. They're a fine breed, Dale. Real fine. And Belle's a good mare."

"I can't wait to meet her."

"Well, since that's got to wait for morning, and it might take awhile for me to get my fill of you, you just might be late for that appointment."

"Well, I reckon the man I came to see about that horse won't mind too much," she quipped, stroking a little firmer. "But I'm curious, Ty. What do you do besides ranching and getting divorced?"

"Oh, now that's a cheap shot," he said with a laugh. "But since it's coming from someone who's two strikes down herself, I'll let it pass. I used to rope a little. But now that I'm getting on in age—"

"Getting on?" she interrupted. "Just how 'getting on' are you?"

"Old. Be forty-four next month."

Dale laughed at the wink he gave her. "Honey, you're talking to a gal who's on the shady side of forty, so unless you're aiming to insult me, don't be going on about forty-something being old."

"You're in your forties?"

"Just turned forty-two last month."

"No."

Dale was sure he was trying to flatter her. She didn't have illusions about herself. She was still in good shape and not ready for the old-folks home by any stretch of the imagination, but she wasn't a young woman and didn't try to appear to be.

"You don't have to flatter me, cowboy. I'm still gonna pay that outrageous price you're demanding for Belle."

Tyler stroked his hand up the side of her neck to cup her face. "Dale, honey, one thing that's a true fact is that I don't ever flatter. Not to get my way, I mean. That's one of my faults, to hear my mama talk. I don't know how to tell them pretty lies women like to hear. I say what I mean. And I mean what I say. And I'm telling you now, that the first look I got at you, I had you pegged for mid-thirties at the oldest. So darlin', when I tell you that you look damn good, it's just a fact."

She couldn't resist the temptation. He was too sexy and she'd been without a man too long. She leaned forward, staring him straight in the eyes. "I appreciate that, Ty. I like honesty. And because I do, I'm gonna tell you that I didn't think you were a boy. I figured you to be close to forty. You've got that look about you that boys try to achieve but fall short of. But even if you were twenty-five or sixty-five, you'd still be sin in jeans."

"God almighty," he breathed and pulled her over on top of him. "Say that again, darlin'."

"My pleasure," she whispered against his lips. "Sin in jeans."

With a groan, he claimed her lips. And all thoughts of horses and cattle and what would happen beyond that night faded away.

Chapter Three

∽

"Time for the seventh inning stretch, handsome," Dale said as she rolled off the bed and onto her feet. She tossed him the wet hand towel lying on the nightstand then gathered her sweat-dampened hair up on top of her head. "God, it's hot."

She walked over to the air conditioning unit and checked the settings. "Damn, what I wouldn't give to be neck deep in the lake back home."

"Like the water do you?"

"Love it."

"So what would you be wearing in this lake back home, honey?"

She turned and gave him a wicked smile. "Nothing."

"Hmmm, and would you be alone?"

"Oh no, you'd be there, cowboy."

"And I'd be wearing?"

"Me."

Ty groaned and closed his eyes then abruptly sat up and grinned. "Well, there's no lake but there is a pool."

"A public pool," she added.

"With no one in it," he corrected as he cleaned himself of the remnants of their last bout of mind-blowing sex. "Not this time of the night."

Dale glanced at the clock. He was right. It was well past the witching hour. "So are you suggesting we go skinny dipping in the hotel pool?"

"Yeah."

She considered it for a moment then ran to the bathroom and grabbed towels. "Here." She tossed one to him and wrapped another around her body.

Ty rose, wound the towel around his waist and, giggling like kids, they left the room and hurried down the hall. Luckily for them, the exit to the pool area did not lie in sight of the front desk.

As he'd predicted, the pool was deserted. There were no lights except for that which filtered in through the palms that circled it from the pole lamps that dotted the parking lot.

Dale wasted no time dropping her towel and diving in. The water was cool and felt wonderful. She surfaced to see Ty standing by the edge of the pool watching.

"Damn, you're sexy wet," he said and dropped his towel and dived in.

Dale resisted the urge to squeal like a teenage girl when he swam over to her and grabbed her legs to pull her under. His hands worked up her legs, skimmed over her hips and wrapped around her waist to pull her to him.

She couldn't remember ever kissing under water but it was a sure bet she'd not easily forget this kiss. Breath held, cool water enveloping their bodies and the hot warmth of his mouth locked with hers, tongue exploring and tasting.

The only thing disappointing in the kiss was having to end it to surface for air. Ty kept his arms around her, paddling her over to the edge of the pool beneath the low diving board. Dale reached up to hang onto the board and wrapped her legs around Ty's waist as he moved his hands up to hold onto the end of the board.

He grinned as her sex pressed against him, pinning his erection between them. "Hey now, you fixing to start trouble?" he warned in a sexy whisper.

"Fixing to?" She wiggled against him. "Cowboy, you started trouble the moment you dropped that towel."

"Well hell, then I'm just gonna have to finish what I started."

Dale gasped as he reached between them and rubbed the head of his cock against her then pushed inside. She almost moaned but he silenced her with a kiss.

It was water gymnastics of the most erotic kind. Ty braced his feet against the wall of the pool, letting her raise and lower herself on him at her own pace. At first she moved slow, savoring the feel of the length of him hilting deep inside her then slowly pulling out. But before long the need to ride him hard and fast had water splashing all around them.

She wasn't paying any attention to the splashes or the surroundings. All her focus was on the build-up of an orgasm that had her humming like a taut string. Just as the sensations started to crest, a loud voice boomed out.

"Hey, what're you doing? Pool closes at ten p.m."

Dale saw Ty's eyes widen then a grin split his face. "Sorry," he called out over his shoulder. "We'll be right out."

Watching over Ty's shoulder, Dale saw the man standing at the door. He hesitated for a moment then turned and went inside. She buried her face against Ty, shaking with laughter and feeling him do the same.

"Come on," he said as their fit of giggles subsided. "I don't think I want to end up in jail buck-naked."

"Amen," she agreed.

They swam over to where they'd left their towels and got out, quickly wrapping the towels around them. Ty chuckled as she hurried to the door. They reached her room and she turned with a look of alarm. "Oh shit!"

"What?"

"I didn't bring the keycard."

Ty laughed. "It's not that funny," she said. "One of us has to go to the front desk for another keycard."

"One of us?" he teased. "Honey, I'm not registered."

"Shit on a stick!" she grumbled. "Fine."

Hitching her towel up and tucking it tightly closed in front, she marched down the hall.

There was only one person manning the front desk. A man aged thirty-something. "Excuse me," Dale said to get his attention.

He looked over at her and his eyes widened. "Yes? Can I help you?"

"I seem to have locked myself out of my room."

The man's mouth tightened in what looked like an attempt to stifle a smile. "I see. Your name?"

"R.D. Evans. Room 107."

He turned his attention to the computer. "Yes, here you are. Just one second."

Dale shifted her weight from one foot to the other and the man created another card for her. He handed it to her with a straight face. "Is there anything else I can do for you, Ms. Evans?"

"No thanks."

"Very well, enjoy your night."

The way he said it made her pause and look him square in the eye. He smiled and she knew he had to be the same man who'd caught her and Ty in the pool. She returned the smile. "I certainly will. Thanks."

Ty was leaning against the wall beside the door when she returned. "Any trouble?"

"Not a bit," she replied and unlocked the door.

"You're something, Dale. Marching down that hall like you were wearing your Sunday best." He grabbed her towel before the door was closed and pulled it off her.

She laughed and made a grab for his towel. "Best birthday suit I own, cowboy."

"Damn fine one too," Ty said as he tossed the towel he held toward the bed.

Dale snorted as she started drying her hair, wringing it out in the towel. "You're one smooth talker, Ty."

"I'm serious as a heart attack, honey." He walked to her, took hold of her upper arms and steered her over in front of the mirror that hung above the dresser.

"Look."

Dale looked into the mirror, seeing their reflection. "Yeah, I see."

Ty nuzzled the top of her shoulder, creating a fresh wave of sensation that rippled over her skin. "No, you don't. Not what I see. Watch."

She bit back an argument as he moved her hair away from her neck, running his tongue lightly over her skin. His hands moved to cup her breasts, making her nipples pucker in anticipation. The moment his thumbs stroked over the hardened peaks, she closed her eyes and leaned back against him.

"Honey, open your eyes. I want you to see what I do to you."

It wasn't just the words he spoke but the tone of his voice. Rough and low and filled with desire. It was the aural equivalent of an aphrodisiac and she had no power to resist.

"Now spread your legs, honey, and put your hands flat on the dresser."

Dale pressed her hands flat on the glossy surface of the dresser and stepped her feet to the sides, a little more than shoulder width, all the while keeping her eyes glued on the reflection of his face in the mirror.

His eyes moved from her reflection and ran over the back of her body as he drifted one hand slowly down her back, over the curve of her ass and in between her legs to softly stroke her sex.

Her breath hitched in her throat, as much from the lusty expression on his face as from his touch. When his free hand moved around her to capture one breast, pinching the nipple lightly between finger and thumb, her breath exploded in a soft gasp.

"Your eyes darken when you feel pleasure," he murmured. "The gold gives way to the darker brown like sun giving way to night."

His fingers worked their way inside her wet channel as he spoke. "And when you start to come, the color deepens to the look of walnut, dark and rich."

Dale had a hard time focusing on his words as his fingers stroked in and out, rhythmic and slow, but deep. Her eyes met his in the mirror and she pushed back against his hand, riding his fingers.

"That's it, darlin'." His voice was a rasped whisper, his eyes taking on the deep hues of a thundercloud just before a storm. "Come for me."

A few more strokes and she couldn't have held back if she'd wanted to. "Ty," she gasped.

"Look at me."

The moment her eyes met his in the mirror the orgasm crested. The desire to close her eyes, let the sensations erase all other aspects of reality was strong. But not as strong as the hold his eyes had on her.

It was unlike any climax she'd experienced before. Locked in his gaze, she was a prisoner, exposed and vulnerable. It was intoxicating and added more dimension to the moment than she'd thought possible.

When at last the wave passed, he smiled at her. "My god, Dale. You're so beautiful."

"It's in the eye of the beholder," she replied and turned to face him.

She met his lips eagerly, pressing against him as he claimed her lips. The taste of him mixed with her sweetness into a blend that was pretty damn intoxicating.

Her body began to grind against him in a way that had his pulse racing like a galloping stallion. The smell of her sex rose in the air, luring him as sure as a fish to bait. Damn, this woman was potent.

He walked her backward, still locked in the kiss, until her legs were pressed against the bed. Then he lowered her down. She broke free of the kiss and straddled his body, rocking on his erection that was trapped between them.

"Honey, being a rancher, you ever hear the term 'ride the wild bull'?"

Dale laughed and gave him a sassy reply, "Why darling, you're talking to the Union County mechanical bull champeen three years running."

Ty let out a whoop and pulled her down for another kiss that nearly set his leg hair on fire. When she rose back up, her hands moved between them to take hold of him. Raising her hips, she rubbed the head of his cock against her wetness then slowly sank down on him.

With a sigh of pleasure, Ty took hold of her hips. "Damn, you feel good."

"Hmmmm," she hummed with a sexy smile and started moving on him. Slowly at first then increasing her pace as his hands tightened on her hips. In minutes the intensity was as high as it could get, both of them bucking and straining, sweat glistening on their skin and breaths coming fast and hard.

"Oh!" She gasped as her pussy started to clench on him. "Can't—stop—ahhhh!" With a groan she threw back her head and rode him even faster. He watched in lust-filled fascination as her body tensed, bowed back and quivered. A throaty moan escaped her right before he felt the warm flush of wetness from her orgasm.

When her body relaxed and she leaned over him, bracing herself on her hands to nip his chin, he grinned. "You done, darlin'?"

"Hell no," she said with a smile then moved off him, rolling onto her back and stretching like a cat. "You're damn near addictive, Ty. Normally I'm a two-shot gal, but you…you inspire all kinds of wicked and lascivious fantasies."

"Lascivious?" He rolled over and propped up on one elbow. "I like the sounds of that. Care to elaborate on that, honey?"

Dale smiled and stretched again. "Like being trussed up and fucked three ways from Sunday or being treated like a bad little girl and having my ass spanked. Or…" she paused and looked him in the eyes with the most sultry expression he'd ever seen. "Having you mount me like a stallion and wearing my butt out."

Ty's heart literally pounded in his chest and his balls tightened so fast and hard it was almost painful. She'd just put into words fantasies he'd never spoken aloud. But she spoke them without hesitation.

Ty grabbed her arm and hauled her to her feet, his lips crushing down on hers in a kiss that had her fisting his thick hair and beginning a plunder of her own. God, he tasted good. Even after all the sex they'd had tonight, just his kiss was enough to trigger her hormones into a frenzied dance.

He had her in his arms, his lips searing hers as he backed her toward the bathroom. She resisted. "The bed," she murmured against his lips.

"Nuh-uh," he argued. "Shower. Like you said, wicked fantasies. And this is one I've been thinking about for a long time. Now come on, get your sweet ass in the shower."

Something about the way he said it, a hint of command in his voice, had a thrill running through her. "Or what?" she teased, running her hand down his body to fist his hard cock.

The smile he gave her was the most deliciously wicked thing she'd ever seen. He wrapped both arms around her, cupping her ass to pull her against him. "I guess I'll just have to turn you over my knee and give you a good spanking."

She nearly came right then and there, but the game was way too much fun to lose her cookies before they even got out of the gate. "Really? And I suppose you think I'm just going to let you?"

She accompanied the tease by rubbing her sex against his cock, feeling the erotic thrill of the coarse hair surrounding it abrade her clit.

His fingers dug into her ass and pulled him even tighter against him. "Oh yeah, honey. I sure do. I think you're not going to just let me, but before I'm done, you're going to beg me."

"Hmmm, promises, promises," she countered a second before his lips claimed hers. Still locked in the kiss, he walked her into the shower. She gasped when he turned on the water and the icy spray rained down on them.

He just laughed and held her squirming against him until the water warmed. Then he turned her back to the spray and knelt down in front of her. "Spread your legs."

As soon as she did, she felt his tongue lapping the length of her sex. "You taste so good. Sweet as honey. Turn around, darlin', so I can get to you better."

She turned and bent at the waist so that her pussy was at his eye level, the warm water beating down on her back and running over her ass. He spread her legs wider and started licking her, sucking the outer lips of her pussy until they felt heavy and swollen. His tongue dipped inside her wet channel, probing and teasing.

She was hugging the wall inside a minute. Every few seconds his tongue would move from her vagina to her clit, making her moan and press back against him. She could feel the vibration begin in her belly, knowing that she was just moments away from coming.

"Oh yes!" she cried, and then groaned in protest when he moved away.

"It's so rude to leave a girl stranded like that," she complained and turned around to see him soaping his hands.

"Stand with your back against the wall."

She wasn't sure what he had in mind, but obeyed anyway. She was literally quivering with arousal, her nipples puckered and hard and her pussy wet from more than just the water from the shower.

He started on her shoulders, working his slick hands slowly down her arms then up again. When he reached her breasts and palmed her nipples in slow circles, she moaned.

The moan was muffled by his mouth in a plundering kiss that was all tongue and teeth. She let him enjoy his invasion for a while then took control, fisting both hands in his hair to feed off him.

The slow burn that had started in her nipples had already escalated into a raging fire that was spreading out from those sensitive buds, making her arch against him. His dick pressed against her belly, throbbing and hard.

She reached down to take his dick in one hand and cup his balls with the other. "Hmmm." She bit at his lip when he moved away from the kiss. He took hold of her wrists to force her hands from him.

"My fantasy, sugar, and I call the shots. Now I'm giving the orders and you don't do anything unless I say so."

She smiled up at him. "And what if I'm bad?"

"Well, I reckon I'm going to have to give you that spanking sooner than I realized."

At first she thought he was just teasing, but when he turned her to face the wall and said, "Bend over, baby," she realized it was no tease.

144

The sexy rasp of his voice was as much of a turn-on as his demands. She bent over and braced her hands on the shower wall. The first smack on her ass made her jump. The second sent a sexual charge though her. He spanked her slowly and precisely, each lash ending with a caress.

After ten smacks she was squirming. Her ass cheeks felt like they were on fire and her pussy felt like an inflated balloon between her legs. On one level, she wanted him to stop. But some unexplored part of her sexual nature wanted more. "Please," she breathed.

"Please what?" He paused, running one hand between her legs to stroke the wet folds of her pussy while the other hand squeezed her ass. "Please, I want more?"

"Yes, more. Please. More."

"Then bend your legs for me. That's it, just a little more. Now spread your legs, babe. That's good. Bend forward just a little more. I want your ass up and open."

She'd just gotten herself into position when he penetrated her ass with his finger. The sensation was as potent as a jolt of electricity. It ran straight through her body and took up residence in her pussy. She cried out then inhaled sharply as his soap-slicked finger probed inside her ass.

"Christ, you're tight. Tight and hot."

She could only moan as he probed in and out, each time going deeper. Her clit was throbbing madly. She reached between her legs to fondle herself and he slapped her ass with a strong smack.

"Not yet," he said. "I'll tell you when to come. If you need something to do with your hands, then reach back here and spread your ass wider for me. This tight little ass of yours is going to take some time to loosen up enough for me to fuck you."

Dale was no babe in the woods, but she'd also never had anal sex and the idea of it was electrifyingly erotic. She followed his command, her fingers digging into the cheeks of her ass as he inserted two fingers inside her.

"That's it, baby," he crooned. "Spread it wide. Come on now, relax your asshole. You're so fucking tight."

She wasn't sure how much more she could take. The sting of the soap added to the unique combination of pleasure and pain, making her damn near close to coming just from being finger-fucked up the ass. Her pussy pulsed, her clit throbbed and her breath rasped as he started to work three fingers inside her.

She felt like she was stretched to the maximum. It was almost too much. Of what, she wasn't sure. The pain and pleasure seemed to be linked.

"Come on, baby, loosen up for me," he crooned in a lover's tone.

"I'm trying. It's too much. I can't take it."

"Yes you can, baby. And you will. Just go with it."

"I can't," she moaned. "It's…"

"Exactly what you want. What I want. You want to give me what I want, don't you?"

"Yes!"

"Then give it to me. Beg me to fuck you up the ass while you masturbate and come. I want you to come for me, honey."

"Please."

"Please what? Say it." His voice was rough with passion.

"Please fuck me up the ass. Now!"

She groaned as he removed his fingers and pressed his cock inside, the muscles protesting at the invasion. "Loosen up, baby."

He pressed slow and steady, feeling her stretch to accommodate him, sliding slowly inside her. The groan that came from her when he pushed deeper was one of longing and surrender, one that robbed him of reason and control. He grabbed her by the hips and pulled her ass to him, impaling her on his length.

She cried out but moved against him, offering him all that he wanted. He stroked slowly, easing out just an inch or so then pressing deep. He knew she struggled to accommodate him, knew that he was taking what she'd offered to no one else. That alone was enough to start the tremors in his belly as an orgasm started to swell.

He tried to prolong it, to move slow and easy, but the need was too great. She was his and the male inside demanded that he take her.

His breath came faster and harder as climax threatened to overwhelm him. "Baby, I can't hold it."

With a groan he exploded, his dick pulsing as he shot deep inside her. She screamed as an orgasm rocked her, her body rolling and bucking.

Chapter Four

ΕΟ

It was near dawn when Ty rolled off Dale, breathing hard, sweaty and with a satisfied smile on his face. He'd had a lot of women in his life, but he'd never experienced anything like what he'd felt with Dale.

Uninhibited and enthusiastic, she could go from being an untamed hell cat to a soft and compliant submissive at the drop of a hat, fulfilling every damn fantasy he'd ever had. And she could laugh and poke fun at him and herself along the way, enjoying sex every bit as much while she was giggling as while she was screaming his name in the midst of an orgasm.

But what shook him was the way she made him feel. They'd loved and talked and argued and wrestled around and loved some more. And he was as happy talking or arguing with her as he was sunk inside her liquid warmth, feeling her tremble against him.

He'd promised himself after his last disaster of a marriage that he wasn't going to step into that swamp again. He still stunk from his last fall into those dark waters. But Dale. Dale made him want to think about it.

Was it possible to fall in love with someone in just one night? If someone had asked him yesterday he'd have said hell no. But now? Now it was different and that unsettled him.

He rolled over and gave her a soft kiss. "I gotta hit the trail, darlin'."

"No, don't go. Not yet," she murmured sleepily.

"Have to, baby. Got stock to tend to and a big appointment today. Some North Carolina gal's driving all the way down here to see me about a horse."

She smiled and kissed him. "Ten o'clock."

"Don't be late."

"Never." She closed her eyes then immediately opened them. "Ty?"

"Yeah, baby?"

"Thank you. This was…special."

He kissed her again, lingering this time. "For me too. See you in a few hours."

Dressing quickly, he let himself out. He should be bone tired, but at the moment felt like a young buck. Even with the unsettled feeling that persisted in his gut. He told himself he'd get over it. Just get on with the day and let things swirl around in the subconscious awhile.

With a light step he left the hotel and walked out into the parking lot, headed for his truck.

Dale opened her eyes when she heard the door close. "Ty?" She looked around. No sign of him. But his phone lay on the bed.

"Aw crap." She grabbed her jeans and slid them on, snatched a tank top from her bag, her keycard and his phone and hustled out of the room. Maybe she could catch him.

She ran out of the hotel and into the parking lot. His truck was still there. She picked up her pace, but as she reached the back of the truck she came to a sudden stop.

Ty stood by the truck door with his hands raised. A man stood in front of him with a gun pointed at Ty's belly.

"Give me the fucking keys and your wallet or I'll fucking shoot you, you fucking cowboy."

Possibilities raced through Dale's mind. Call 9-1-1? It would probably alert the gunman. And the police couldn't get there fast enough. Yell and hope it scared him away? No, he might shoot Ty.

149

Damn! If only she had a weapon. Suddenly a crazy notion appeared in her mind and her hand went to her pocket. It was still there. The rock the woman had given her. She pulled it out, hearing Ty respond to his assailant.

"No need to get riled," Ty said calmly. "I'll give you want you want, but to do that, I'm gonna have to lower my hands."

Dale sucked in her breath. She'd nailed more than one snake and a whole lot of tin cans with rocks. But could she hit a man hard enough to keep him from hurting Ty? Only one way to find out.

Ty watched the man's eyes. He was obviously jacked up on something. Nervous as a June bug at a duck reunion. "You make one fucking move," the man warned, "and—" The last sound out of his mouth was a grunt as something slammed into his temple and he pitched sideways then down onto his knees, his eyes rolling wildly in his head.

Ty started to make a grab for the gun, but before he could someone slammed into the man and sent him tumbling. Dale. The man hit the ground and rolled onto his back, dazed and bloody from the cut on his head. He waved the gun unsteadily.

Ty kicked at the man's hand and the man squeezed off a shot that went wild, up into the air. Dale landed on the man's gut, straddling him. She grabbed his wrist in both hands and slammed it down on the pavement. The gun discharged and the shot sounded louder than any Ty had ever heard.

"You son of a bitch!" Dale shouted and pounded his hand on the pavement again.

The man took a swing at her with his free hand, but Ty intercepted, grabbing his arm and twisting it sharply. The man screamed but Ty didn't let go.

Neither did Dale stop slamming the man's hand on the pavement until the gun fell from his grip. She let go with one hand and knocked the gun out of his reach, then balled up her fist, reared back and punched him square in the nose.

A howl accompanied the sound of a loud crunch. Ty grabbed her and yanked her up off the man, who rolled over, clutching his face and bellowing like a wounded buffalo.

Dale turned to him with wild eyes, her hands patting rapidly over him. "Are you okay? He didn't hurt you, did he? You're not shot?"

"I'm fine. I'm fine." He grabbed her hands to still them. "Honey, it's fine."

"Oh damn." She fell against him, hugging him tightly. "I was so scared. I thought he was going to...to shoot you and —"

The rest of her words were incomprehensible as she lapsed into sobs, heaving against him, her face buried against his chest.

"It's okay, darlin', it's okay," he crooned, keeping an eye on the moaning man on the ground. "Now I need you to let go so I can call the police and —"

They both looked around at the sound of sirens. A few seconds later flashing lights could be seen on the road leading to the hotel. It wasn't long before three police cars skidded to a stop and officers jumped up, guns leveled at Dale and Ty over the tops of their cars.

"It's okay." Ty held up his hands. "No weapons."

"Ma'am," one of the officers shouted. "You need to raise your hands slowly."

Dale raised her hands and after a couple of seconds, one of the officers walked over to them while the other two kept their weapons trained on them.

"Ty?" the officer asked.

"Hey, Mike," Ty greeted him.

Mike yelled over his shoulder to his partners. "Clear!"

One of them picked up the gun from the pavement while the other radioed for an ambulance.

"What happened here, Ty?"

"I was leaving to head home and that fella stuck a gun in my gut and asked for my keys and money."

"And you obviously didn't feel obliged to comply."

"Wasn't me. This little gal beaned him with a rock in the side of the head then jumped on him and stomped the crap outta him."

"You?" The officer looked at Dale.

"Yes, sir."

He looked from her to Ty and burst out laughing. "I take it you two know each other?"

"Yep."

The officer shook his head, still chuckling. "Well, I'm gonna need the both of you to give statements."

"No problem."

"Okay, let me deal with this first."

"We'll wait right here."

The officer moved away and Ty pulled Dale to him, putting one finger beneath her chin to tilt her head up. "You're something, Dale Evans."

"Not really."

"Yes, really. You might've just saved my life, Dale. Damn, woman, where the hell did you learn to throw like that? And where the hell did you find a rock?"

"The rock!" She looked around scanning the pavement. "We have to find the rock."

"Honey, it's just a—"

"No, Ty. We have to find the rock."

"Okay, okay."

In the end, they and two of the officers searched for the rock for an hour as they gave their statements. She finally found it, underneath a nearby car.

"You sure that's it?" Ty asked.

"Yes, positive. Thank you." She looked around gratefully at the police officers. "Thank all of you."

"I think Ty ought to be thanking you," Mike said. "You might just have saved his sorry hide."

"Thanks, Mike," Ty said good-naturedly. "You got all you need from us?"

"Yeah."

"Then let's get you back inside so you can clean up and get some sleep," Ty said to Dale, wrapping his arm around her waist to turn her toward the hotel.

"Thanks for helping me look for the rock," she said and put her arm around him, their steps falling into rhythm with one another.

"No problem, honey. Least I could do."

As they neared the door, he looked down at her. "Out of curiosity, just what's so special about that rock?"

Just then the hotel door opened and the woman who'd given her the rock stepped out. A long black limo was waiting at the curb with a liveried driver standing by the back door holding it open.

"She gave it to me," Dale said and stepped into the woman's path. "Excuse me?"

"Hello, my dear," the woman said with a smile, and looked at Tyler for a moment. "I see that your visit has proven...eventful."

"This rock. Why did you give it to me?"

The woman looked at her for a long moment then smiled. "Once, many years ago in my homeland, there was a great society of women who fought to save the world. In one of their many battles, a great man was saved, a man who went on to do great good in the world. Each woman who fought that day took from the battlefield a rock. A remembrance that some things are worth fighting for, worth dying for. That rock belonged to one of those women."

"Really?" Dale looked down at the rock then offered it to the woman. "Then you should take it back. It's...it's too important to give it to me."

"On the contrary, my dear. Any woman who has the courage to fight to save the life of another is a warrior equal to the heroes of old. "She glanced at Ty. "Just as any man willing to dedicate his life to the preservation of a noble species is someone who affects the world for the better."

Dale looked at Ty whose mouth was hanging open. "What're you talking about?" he asked.

The woman smiled and walked to the door of the limo then paused and looked back at them. "When the Spanish came to this world, they introduced something new to the continent. A magnificent breed of horse, strong and intelligent. They nearly perished, their numbers dwindling until they faced sure extinction. But there are those who strive to preserve the line, breathe new life and new numbers into this magnificent breed so that the past does not die but lives on for those who come after us.

"Such a man would be well served to find a mate as passionate about his cause, as willing to sacrifice and fight for what is right as he, wouldn't you say, Mr. Austin?"

Ty gaped at her in shock and Dale looked at her in amazement. "You know a lot about us apparently. But we don't know anything about you. Not even your name."

"Danu," the woman said with a smile. "You may call me Danu. Farewell, Dale Evans. Walk well, my young warrior."

With that, she got in the car. The driver closed the door, tipped his hat to them with a smile then rounded the car, got in and drove off.

Dale and Ty stared after the car, both speechless. Finally Ty turned to her. "That was...hell, I don't know what that was."

"Me either, to be honest," Dale admitted. "But please don't let what she said make you feel like you're obligated in any way to —"

"Stop," Ty interrupted. "Don't say it. Maybe this is one of those things my mom would say is best left unexplained. A portent or sign."

"A portent? Is your mom a witch or something?"

"Maybe. A little," he said with a chuckle. "Or so my dad says. But the point is, somehow or other you ended up being given a rock by that woman. And you used that rock to save my life. Now whether that was fate or just crazy luck, it still ends up the same. You saved me."

"You wouldn't have needed to be saved if you hadn't met me."

"Maybe. Or maybe this was supposed to happen. To show us both something important."

"Like what?"

"Like the fact that despite how completely insane it is, I feel like I've been waiting for you my whole life, Dale. Just marking time and going through women looking for the right one. And then you showed up. And now…now I think we owe it to ourselves to figure out if that's true."

"Ty, I…god, I'd so love to believe that. Maybe even part of me does. But I'm scared shitless of marriage and I don't want to make another mistake."

"Me either. But there's no law that two people have to sign a piece of paper to bind them to one another. Love is supposed to be what keeps people together."

"That's what I hear," she said with a smile.

"So, Ms. Evans, any chance you could come to love a broke-down old cowboy from Kissimmee who raises Cracker horses and doesn't give a hoot in hell for shopping, fancy dressing and ritzy restaurants?"

Dale stepped up to him and looped her arms around his neck. "That depends, Mr. Austin."

"On what?"

"On where all this love is gonna take place. North Carolina or Kissimmee?"

A sexy smile came on Ty's face. "Tell you what. Let's get on back to your room and I'll wrestle you for it."

"Best two out of three?"she asked teasingly.

"Best however many you want, honey. Just promise me you won't leave 'til we get this figured out?"

She considered it for a moment. The place back home had more than enough people to see to it. In fact, her brothers would probably stand up and cheer to have her out of their hair for a while. And it'd been a long time since she'd taken a chance and tried something new, somewhere new.

"Tell you what," she finally said. "You come on back to my room and we'll...negotiate."

"Negotiate?" He raised his eyebrows. "Naked?"

"Why, honey, is there any other way?"

Ty laughed and hugged her tight, swinging her up off her feet. "I got the feeling that we're gonna raise some fine horses together, Dale Evans."

"And I got a feeling we're gonna raise more than that," she teased. "If you got the stamina for another round."

"Whisper the secret code in my ear and I'm yours, honey."

"Sin in jeans," she breathed into his ear.

Ty grinned, swung her up in his arms and marched into the hotel. "Hell yeah."

FAE'S GARGOYLE

Sally Painter

ജ

Prologue

ഔ

Myth, magic or legend? There have been Hussies since before time was measured in days and minutes. Women who fought bravely alongside their mates with sword and axe, warriors whose courage changed the world around them. Led by the first Hussy, Danu, these fierce fighters discovered their inner strengths, summoned reserves they didn't know they possessed and passed into the fabric of legend with their daring exploits.

Since that time, myths have been spun around the Hussy Warriors—tales told by firelight, whispered from mother to daughter—eventually to take their place amongst the mystical fables that shape our souls.

But the essence of a Hussy remains strong in the hearts of so many women. Heroines who don't realize that within them lies the power to make a difference, to effect change, to use their passion every bit as skillfully as Danu wielded her sword so long ago. Warriors in different times and different places, who love as deeply and desire as desperately as any woman ever has, seldom knowing that their desire will impact not just one man, but so much more.

Therein lies the magic of a Hussy. To right a wrong, turn a frown to a smile—to positively change those around her. To love a man with every fiber of her body, to learn from that love and to grow stronger because of it.

Whether in the past, the future, or the here-and-now, there are Hussies around each corner. They may not even be aware of their Hussy destiny. But one thing is certain—when passion knocks on their door, lives will change for the better.

159

And when it comes to their one special hero? Well, he's in for the ride of his life.

Which leaves one unanswered question...are *you* a Hussy?

Chapter One

ဢ

Maria Jennings opened her eyes and was startled to find a naked man lying beside her. Her erratic heartbeat pounded in her ears. She jerked up in bed but the painful throbbing in her temple forced her back down onto the pillow. The room spun around her. Swallowing the dryness in her throat, she tried to remember what had happened. How had she ended up here? Naked?

The sound of the ocean pounding outside the open patio door matched the hammering in her head. The last thing she remembered was standing in Danu's castle saying goodbye after months of training. It was time to begin her mission, so why was she naked and in bed with—just who was this man?

Gingerly, she lifted up onto one arm and blinked against the diffused light. The room illuminated brighter each time the silk draperies billowed out and a breeze rushed across the room, carrying the scent of ocean and tropical flowers. Her spirit soared with the smell of home, only something was missing within the familiar scents. Something was very wrong.

Moonlight rushed across the room and fell over the muscular man lying beside her. Shadows swayed and the light moved across indented buttocks, then rose past broad shoulders to stretch toward dark wavy hair. Before she could glimpse his face, the light flittered away with the retreating breeze.

She held her breath and waited until the next gust of wind shoved the draperies aside in a fluttering mass and once more bathed the naked man in soft light. It moved over him like an ocean's tide and this time touched his face.

Her pulse spiked. She sat straight up in bed and smothered a gasp with trembling hands. This had to be a dream!

She was in bed with Denton Prescott!

It couldn't be. She closed her eyes, but when she opened them he was still there. Denton Prescott? In bed with her? Naked? He shifted onto his stomach, turning his back to her. Maria dropped her gaze. Heat rushed to her cheeks. His buttocks were just as fine as she remembered. Well, she'd never seen them in the flesh, only in stone when he'd stood to take flight but had been caught in the rays of sunrise.

The moment rushed back to her as though it happened only yesterday instead of ten years ago. They'd been chatting on the campus steps late into the night. Time had seemed endless until the first rays of daylight struck his face. She'd been in awe as she watched his magnificent gargoyle form emerge and his clothes singe to ash. The hardening had spread over him until he was completely cast in stone.

She released her breath. It seemed an eternity since that night. A painful eternity when he was called to war, never once contacting her. And when he returned home a hero, he was quickly caught up in the life of a celebrity. She stared down at his hard, muscled body, her fingers itching to stroke the fine planes. Instead, she closed her hands into fists. How cruel this was. Her fondest fantasy come true and she was unable to touch him.

Unable to tell him how much she loved him. Not that he cared.

The air stirred cooler and she shivered. What had Danu been thinking, plopping her down into his bed? She had long since tamped down her feelings for him, but at that moment realized when she'd been captured forever. Ever since he'd flashed that first devastating smile.

Oh, Danu, what have you done? Maria shook her head. The ancient guru wasn't a cruel creature so this had to be a mistake. She tried to recall arriving there but met a thick fog where memories should reside.

Regardless how she'd ended up in Denton's bed, she must fly away before he woke up and discovered her. Scooting out of the bed, she bent down and groped at the discarded clothes littering the floor. Her fingers closed around a dark-colored dress but she froze when he stirred again. She scooped up the dress and tiptoed toward the open bedroom door.

Her heartbeat pounded in her ears as she hurried down the hall, all her attention focused on the arched doorway ahead. She emerged into what appeared to be a large den lit by a corner floor lamp. Her bare feet slapped against the terra-cotta tiled floor while she struggled to pull the silk dress over her head. She hurried toward the glass doors, determined to exit through the portico and fly into the night. The ocean sang to her and her pulse pounded like the waves beating against the sand. Just where the hell was she? Nothing seemed familiar. The gardens surrounding the pool were not the rich vibrant colors she was accustomed to seeing. There was no magical vibration in them. In anything.

She'd worry about that later. Right now she needed to escape. She stretched forward, but the familiar pop didn't come. She checked the dress to make sure none of the material was covering her shoulder blades. The strapless garment fit fine. Nothing to block her wings. Again she flexed her muscles and mentally summoned her faerie wings to release.

Nothing.

Okay, maybe she was sick. That might account for her inability to recall how she'd ended up in Denton's bed. Pain seared her temple and she gripped the back of a nearby chair. Oh, that was not normal. She massaged the throbbing ache with trembling fingers. She'd just leave by her own two feet and try flying once she was away from the house.

The image of Denton lying beside her flashed across her mind. Oh dear butterfly wings! She'd been in bed with Denton Prescott. Her breath came in hard, short pants. And she was running away from him because? She mentally shook herself. Because she had no explanation for being there. Because he didn't love her.

But Denton...naked... She wrung her hands together, longing to return to his bed and at long last live out her greatest fantasy. Enough of this. She had to leave before he found her there. She took a deep breath and reached for the door knob.

"Where are you going?" came a groggy baritone voice behind her.

Caught! Her heart skipped a beat. What should she do? She pretended she hadn't heard him and closed her fingers around the knob.

"Baby? Where are you going?"

Her heart was drumming so loudly in her ears she could barely hear but she certainly heard him call her baby.

"Ah...home," she said, not daring to look back at him. "I need to go home."

"But you are home. Did you forget where you are?" His laughter was rich and fell over her like melted chocolate. Her knees weakened. Why would he say she was home?

"I-I..." She mentally shrugged at how lame she sounded and closed her eyes, not daring a glance in his direction.

"It's normal. Sometimes it takes a few days to adjust. Memories can be sketchy until that time." He padded over to her and she found herself engulfed in muscular arms. Her breath hung in her throat.

"P-Please." The word squeaked past the tightening in her throat.

His hard body molded against her, shocking her senses into overdrive. His cock, thick and stiff, pressed into the small of her back. Liquid fire coursed through her. Denton was holding her in his arms. Sexy, naked Denton had called her baby. She could just melt into a pool of lust right there.

"Come back to bed, Missus Prescott."

"What?" The room spun around her.

Strong arms cocooned her and she leaned against him for support lest her legs give out from under her. The only thing she was aware of was his hard body pressed so tightly against hers. Nerve endings tingled and a rush of want seized her.

"It was a beautiful wedding, Maria," he whispered in her ear.

She had married Denton? How? When?

"Oh baby, you are the sexiest woman I've ever known." He nuzzled her neck and delightful shivers cascaded down her.

"I-I..." Her thoughts were jumbled. Each kiss he planted in the hollow of her neck made it impossible to think.

"Hmm, you taste sweet. I can't get enough of you." His heated breath fanned over her. "So where are you off to in the middle of the night?"

"Ah...my house...to get a few things."

He chuckled. "You have such a great sense of humor. I'll take you to a shop in the morning."

"Morning? But...you'll turn to stone if you go out." She pivoted to face him and was instantly lost in crystal-blue eyes. He was just as magnificent as he'd been that morning on campus. The passing years had made him sexier. The most promising warrior-in-training had grown into a mighty...strong...virile... She licked her lips.

He leaned down and covered her mouth with his. Maria quivered. His tongue teased her lips and she relaxed her mouth to receive him. Emotions welled inside her. His kiss deepened and she returned it by twisting her tongue around his.

Oh sweet faerie dust! How often had she dreamed of this moment? She didn't understand what had happened and no longer cared. Denton was kissing her. Firm hands cupped her buttocks and he lifted her to his waist. Her body responded in a rush of want and urgent need. She wrapped her legs around him and the silk dress slipped up her thighs, bunching around her waist.

She startled when his cock, rigid and hot, eased into her opening. Fire singed her nerve endings and a wet heat rushed from her. His cock eased deeper. Her pulse was erratic. Her senses overloaded with the feel of him. His taste. She wanted him to take her. Anticipation throbbed in her. She held her breath as he inched his cock deeper.

He broke from the kiss, panting, and Maria opened her eyes. The look in his eyes burned with the same fire coursing through her. "I just love fucking you," he whispered. "Only it's more than sex, baby. You know that, right? I mean, this is real. I love you so much, Maria."

His words sent a thundering roar through her. Denton loved her. Maria cupped his face between her hands and reached up to kiss him once more. She pressed her lips to his and thrust her tongue into his mouth. He groaned and flicked his tongue around hers.

Large hands tightened around her buttocks and he pressed his cock into her channel. Maria rolled her hips, enjoying the way he filled her. He tasted even better than she'd imagined. Hot and spicy. He leaned against the wall to support them and braced strong legs apart. Slowly he pumped his cock into her.

Maria broke from the kiss, gasping for air. She tossed her head back. Her hair tumbled down her back, plastering to the perspiration that prickled along her back. His flesh was feverish beneath her hands. Hard muscles flexed and didn't budge underneath her grasp.

Each time his cock slipped in and out of her, delightful twinges raced up her spine. The urge for more curled and twisted in a writhing rhythm. She flattened her feet on the wall behind him and met each thrust. Frenetic energy rose higher only to slip back down, teasing her with the promise of release.

She wanted more and quickened her movements. Possessed with the need to take him deeper inside her, Maria rolled her hips, matching each thrust.

He fucked her faster and faster. The building excitement consumed her. A deep-chested groan rumbled from him.

"Oh, Denton," she gasped. Perspiration drenched them. The edgy energy teased her, driving her into a frenzy. She lifted her hips and eased his cock from her so the tip teased her opening.

He mumbled something and strong fingers dug into her flesh as he tugged her back down his length. She lifted again and once more he brought her back down his shaft, tightening his grip.

She tottered on the edge of orgasm. Pleasure teased her with the promise of more. She licked her lips and stretched backward, longing to feel the intensity of release. He pulled his cock out and then plunged past the folds of her opening.

"Oh sweet paradise, Maria."

His muscles flexed underneath her fingers. Fire lashed at her clit. His hands slid around her waist and underneath her dress, pulling the thin material up as he slipped the dress over her head and arms. Free of the confining silk, her breasts crushed against his chest. The contact of his flesh to hers sent her pulse throbbing. Their bodies stuck together in a seal of heat and perspiration. She lowered her legs from the wall, easing them around his waist.

He slowed his rhythm long enough to bury his head into her breasts and close his lips around one nipple. He suckled the tender bud, rolling his tongue around the sensitive nub. Quicksilver flashes throbbed to her clit. Her hands glided over hard muscles, wet from sweat.

"I want to make you scream my name," he said, and suddenly shifted from the wall. He carried her over to the dining table and the marble top greeted her ass. The contrast of the sudden cold against her flesh was erotic. He planted his hands beside her head.

"Denton," she murmured, tilting her hips to better receive him. The image of him leaning over her with snips of moonlight glistening on his dark hair made her pulse jump. "I love you, Denton."

He groaned and pounded his cock into her pussy. The sound of his balls slapping against her ass echoed around them and Maria lifted her legs higher, encircling his neck. This seemed to incite him and he tugged her into each thrust.

Wildfire coursed through her. It streaked up her spine and rushed to her head. The orgasm exploded, seizing her in a series of molten sensations and spasms. The walls of her pussy clamped around his cock. "Denton!"

His body went rigid and he reared back, groaning. His cum erupted hot inside her and she released the ankle-lock, allowing her legs to slide to his waist.

"Maria." He nuzzled her neck. Heated pants fanned over her and Maria felt as though she had turned to liquid and soaked into him.

Making love to Denton was better than anything she'd imagined. She sighed. Years of pining for him were gone. Old pain transformed into joy.

At long last her wish had come true. Denton loved her.

Chapter Two

∞

"My beautiful Maria." Denton lifted his head and smiled down at her. "I do so love you."

She could feel his cock throbbing inside her and closed her eyes, willing their lovemaking to be real. She couldn't endure the heartache if she awoke and discovered it had all been just another vivid dream.

He leaned down to suckle her breasts. His tongue rolled over a nipple and he sucked the hardened bud into his mouth. Pulses throbbed to her clit and spent passions reawakened.

"Denton," she panted. She was unable to think. Unable to move. All she could say was his name. Over and over again.

He massaged her other breast and she relaxed against the need to ask him how she'd ended up in his bed. And when they'd been married. A smile spread over her lips, parting into a wide grin she didn't try to control. She was married to Denton Prescott! This was truly paradise. She sighed, enjoying the thought until…realization barged in. This might be Danu's magic. She stiffened and he lifted his head. A dark frown creased his handsome face.

"What's wrong, baby?"

Maria eased from him and his cock scraped free of her pussy. She slid from the table and stumbled across the room to retrieve her dress. She let the silky waves fall over her hips and then turned to face him, slightly embarrassed, unsure what to do now that she'd so thoroughly made love to him.

Yet she reminded herself there was nothing to fear. Denton loved her. If she could trust his love was real. Her deepest hope had finally come true.

"Why did you get dressed?"

"I'm sorry, Denton. I just…" She pressed her fingertips to her temple. "You see… Well, I don't remember getting married. I know that sounds crazy." She ran her hand through her hair, glancing over at him. "Do you remember?"

His forehead creased. "Of course I remember. It was the happiest moment in my life."

"I don't recall much of anything. Not how I got here or…"

"It's okay, Maria. I had a hard time adjusting when I first arrived." He closed the distance between them and she found herself enveloped in his arms once more. She tingled each place his body touched hers. And when she met his dark gaze all resistance disappeared. "Maybe you had too much tequila tonight. I'm sorry. I should have stopped you after the first two drinks, but you were having so much fun celebrating our marriage and I thoroughly enjoyed watching you dance like that."

"Dance?" she asked, desperately trying to recall the event. She'd married him and participated in a celebration yet couldn't recall it. This was one powerful spell to place such details into his mind.

Laughter echoed around her. Scenes of dancing with Denton teased her but faded back into the fog. A little tropical chapel emerged from the drunken recesses of her mind, followed by a scene of a druid priest. She felt disconnected to the scenes as though they'd happened to someone else. Her breathing quickened.

"Are we on the coast of Enchanted Albia?" she asked.

"Baby, don't you remember how you got here?" He frowned at her.

She shook her head.

"You really don't remember our wedding?" He ran his finger down her arm.

She stared at him, not wanting to hurt his feelings.

"Remember how I got the priest out of bed to perform the ceremony? I promised to give him a big donation." He dropped a tender kiss on her shoulder.

She tried to recall but it was difficult to concentrate when he kept touching her.

"Surely you remember, baby. It was your idea to get married tonight." His blue eyes widened. Hope glinted in their depths and it would quickly be replaced with pain if she told him the truth. The last thing she wanted to do was cause her beloved Denton any distress.

"Yes...I...it's a bit broken." Perhaps she'd remember later, once her mind cleared.

"Yep, too much tequila." His face broke into a wide grin.

Staring up at him, Maria was overwhelmed. Charisma didn't adequately describe the energy emanating from him. Great faerie kings, was it any wonder he was such a powerful force in the world? With that kind of attraction working for him, who could resist? Surely it was what helped make him so successful. She locked with his gaze. Oh yeah, that smile was enough to disarm and beckon her to forget about the hows and whys and just enjoy being with him.

Pain seared her temple and she leaned forward to rest her head on his chest. Strong hands stroked her hair and somehow his touch soothed the ache. Was that part of his magic? She'd heard gargoyles had the power to heal, but thought it merely myth.

"Come over here and sit down." Denton led her to the leather couch and sat down beside her.

"I'll be okay. Maybe some water?" The words barely squeaked past the dryness in her throat and she closed her eyes, willing her memory to return, but it fluttered just beyond reach.

"I have bottled water." He jumped up and disappeared through an archway to what she assumed must be a kitchen.

171

Maria held her hands to her head and leaned forward, trying to make the room stop spinning. Her stomach roiled with a queasy feeling. She was going to be sick but fought the rising bile. Instead, she trained her thoughts on the mission. Danu's last words still rang in her ears.

Ye must save this man. He is a prisoner, unjustly accused of a deed he did not commit. Ye shall know how to vindicate him when the time comes.

It was absurd. Clearly, Denton was no one's prisoner. How could Danu be so wrong?

"Here you go," he said, handing her the chilled water bottle while he settled beside her. "You are so beautiful, my love." He lifted a long strand of hair from her face and smoothed it over her shoulder.

Maria gulped the cold liquid. It ran down her parched throat and she felt as though she'd walked out of a desert and plunged into a cool spring.

"You're dehydrated. Need another?"

She shook her head and finished the bottle.

"You've made me so happy, Maria. I thought my life was over and then there you were, standing on the beach."

"Why would your life be over?" She blinked up at him and met a loving look. Something about him was different. He wasn't the same brusque, war-driven soldier she so vividly recalled being interviewed and honored a few years ago. Danu must be right. Something had happened to him.

"We've not talked much since first meeting this morning. My fault." He chuckled.

She surmised they'd been too busy making love. She should at least recall that.

"Do you remember how we bumped into each other on the beach this morning?"

A scene flashed in front of her. She'd found herself in the red dress and high heels, standing on the beach. She could still feel the warm sand under her bare feet as she carried her shoes in one hand. She'd decided to walk up the beach and see what was waiting for her, never suspecting it would be Denton.

"You were asleep on a beach towel."

"Yeah, baby. That's right. To wake up and find you standing over me. I thought I was dreaming."

"I remember." Their conversation came back to her in bits and pieces. "But you were in the sun, Denton. You weren't stone."

"I guess that's one advantage to living here."

She started to ask how he was unaffected by the sun but he continued talking.

"We sat and talked for a while. And when I found out you'd always felt the same way about me as I had you...I mean, I had no idea. That night on campus. We'd talked into the morning hours and I was caught in the sunlight. You stayed with me all day. I didn't tell you then but I'd just received my orders and was transferring out the next night to an outpost in the Yema galaxy. Then the war broke out and I didn't feel it was fair to become involved with you only to leave you behind for no telling how long. It turned out to be five years. During that time I resigned to being without you."

"Oh Denton."

He shook his head and continued talking about the war. His words faded and all she could hear was the melodic rise and fall of his voice. She'd been in love with Denton ever since his family had moved to Dream City. She'd watched him flying at night, often following him undetected.

She'd done everything she could to get him to notice her — well, almost everything — but he was always drawn to the girls who developed their magical skills early and knew how to wrap a boy around their fingers. She didn't want his love like that. A spell eventually wore off. So she'd resigned herself to an unrequited love until the day she died. His words drifted through her musings.

"You should have told me how you felt. We could have worked it out. I thought you were unapproachable as anything other than a friend. I mean, our worlds don't exactly mix. Faeries tend to be pretty closed to inter-relationships. So I watched you from a distance."

"You did?" she asked, snapping back to reality.

He paused to smile down at her. "You still haven't told me how you ended up here. I've not seen a single fae since I arrived a year ago."

"I-I guess it was destiny." Things were becoming clearer but there were still gaps of missing time. "I'm sorry, but it's still a bit fuzzy, Denton," she said.

He ran a finger around her ear. "I love your faerie ears. They really turn me on." He gave her a lopsided grin and her heart throbbed. "I'm just glad we finally got together, even if it was here."

"What's wrong with here?" She looked around. "It's paradise."

"It is now. You know, it's rare to get a second chance at true love, Maria. And what are the odds we'd both end up here?"

"I...know..." If someone was threatening to imprison him then she must figure out a way to prevent it. She looked at him and thought how absurd it was that a gargoyle warrior would need a fae's help.

The pain in her head eased and more memories flooded past the thinning fog. She'd sat on the beach with him, laughing and talking all morning, reminiscing about school and how their lives had gone in such opposite directions.

When he'd invited her to lunch, Maria knew the sparks flying between them would only heat up once within the privacy of his home. Before she knew what was happening, they were making love. Broken vignettes cascaded on top of each other. Denton had made love to her several times. And that night, while enjoying a romantic dinner at a local restaurant, he'd proposed.

"Are you feeling any better?"

"Somewhat." She nodded.

"What about some fresh air?" he asked and helped her stand.

Maria leaned against him, sensing the power in his solid body, recalling how it felt being possessed by him. A giddy heat radiated through her. The tequila residue no longer impaired her mind and the remaining fragments flooded back to her.

She glanced down, knowing all she had to do was touch him and she'd be reliving the sexual bliss he'd just given her. Instead, she let him open the patio door and stepped onto the portico. She stared past the pool to the ocean. The full moon reflected over the waves like glitter and a balmy breeze lifted her hair from her shoulders. She took a deep breath through her nostrils, the smell of home beckoning her, but again, the scent was disturbing, alien to their world.

"It's a beautiful night," he said and pulled her against him. Maria smiled, cradled in his arms with her back to his chest. She tingled at the feel of his cock pressing against her. "Do you remember everything now?" he asked and kissed her ear.

Goose bumps raced down her back. It was so easy to get lost in his passion and how quickly things had happened between them.

"I want to make love to you again." He buried his head in her hair and turned her around to face him. Blue eyes set beneath perfect male eyebrows widened and her breath rushed from her. He was gorgeous. She trailed her fingers over his arms, loving the way his biceps felt underneath her stroking.

"Oh, Denton," she sighed. "I can't believe this is real."

"Then let me prove it to you." He grabbed her hand and led her to the pool. "Skinny dipping in moonlight. You can't get any more real." Before she could protest, he fell backward into the water.

She watched him go under and then resurface. His laughter rang out into the night.

"Come on, Maria." He splashed water at her.

For a moment, she felt like a teenager again. Skinny dipping was something she'd done once with a group of girls at a sleepover in the Cameronesse Forest. They'd stolen into the hidden garden of the magi and dipped into his magic pool. Denton disappeared under the water and she peeled the dress over her head.

Resurfacing, he shook his head but stopped when his gaze fell on her.

Maria smiled, feeling the heat of his stare. She dove into the pool. The water was cool as she glided through it. She resurfaced with her hair floating around her shoulders. Denton had stopped a few feet away, staring with so much emotion playing over his face, she longed to freeze the moment in time and live in it forever. Tears welled in her eyes. She felt a tug on her heart each time she realized Denton was her husband.

"You look like a sea nymph." He swam over to her.

Maria watched his arms slicing through the water and marveled how magnificent and sleek he was. His dark hair glistened with specks of moonlight. Each time the muscles in his arms flexed in another stroke, her pulse spiked. She swallowed against the rising heat. His brilliant mind and mischievous personality were like magnets to her.

"Come here, you," he said and tugged her to him. The water rushed around her and she draped her arms over his shoulders while her legs drifted around his waist. The water's buoyancy rocked her against him. His hard cock teased her as it bobbed against her. Large hands, warm and wet, stroked her

176

back, and she gazed up into his eyes, instantly lost in a sea of blue.

"I bet you can't catch me," she laughed and twirled out of his arms. She needed a distraction lest she be lost in him forever.

Chapter Three

ဢ

Denton watched his wife swimming away from him. She dipped headfirst into the water and dove underneath the surface. He felt as though his heart stopped when her rounded ass fanned above the water then disappeared with long legs slowly sinking out of sight.

Damn! He was married to Maria Jennings! His heart pounded against his rib cage. How was it possible that she'd ended up on the island too? The world had taken on a magical feel ever since he'd heard her soft, lilting voice say his name. A voice he'd feared never to hear again.

When he'd seen her in that sexy red dress with her hair falling in waves around her shoulders, he'd had an instant hard-on. But what he felt for her went deeper than just physical attraction. Old emotions had sparked to life and burst into a raging wildfire. He couldn't get enough of her.

The moment he kissed her, Denton knew he was going to marry her. And even though he was teasing about stealing away into the night together, she took him up on it without the slightest hesitation. She loved him. Genuinely loved him. Not because of his fame but because of who he was. The real Denton Prescott few ever bothered to get to know. Chaste certainly never troubled herself to know who he was. Had he allowed himself to see beyond the witch's façade, everything would have turned out differently. Of course, then he wouldn't have found Maria again.

Everything has its own design in life. His father's voice rang in his mind. This was the first time Denton had witnessed its unfolding.

Maria resurfaced and he envied the water rolling down her face. Her eyes softened with the same love beating in his heart. Those large brown eyes revealed everything. Innocent. Pure. Trusting. How could he not be seduced?

"You're still as magical as I remember you," he said, swallowing the burning lump forming in his throat.

"I bet you say that to all the faeries." She swam right into his open arms.

Her breasts brushed against him and his body shocked alert. How he loved her soft curves. He held her closer, never wanting to lose the magic of the night.

He nuzzled where her shoulder and neck met and inhaled deeply. Her scent was forever imprinted on him. Her taste. Her touch. When had she become a part of him? Was it the moment he looked up and saw her standing on the beach or was it the first time he made to love to her?

He danced with her in the water, moving to the music playing in his mind. A song that always reminded him of the day she'd spent by his side while he was stone. She'd sung it to him. Over and over.

"What are you humming?" she asked and lifted her head.

He stopped and little eddies moved about them.

"Our song." He cradled the back of her head in his hand. Her lush lips were wet, begging to be kissed. "The song you sang to me." He leaned down and brushed his lips ever so lightly against hers, enjoying how soft her lips were against his.

"Uhm," she murmured.

His breath hung in his chest. He wanted more. He could never get enough of her. She was an addiction. One he intended to enjoy for all eternity. Her arms encircled his neck and she returned the hunger in his kiss, slipping her tongue inside his mouth. Everything about her was exciting. Her fingers closed around his cock and she moved to mount him, pressing the tip of his cock into her opening.

The fleshy lips of her pussy spread open and he eased inside. Her opening was tight as he inched deeper. She rolled her hips and he grasped her by the waist. The raw need to claim her once more was like a rising fever. Frustrated by the water's interference, he eased from her to scoop her up into his arms and carry her toward the underwater steps.

Maria squealed, kicking her legs in mock protest as he climbed up the steps. The water cascaded from them. He headed for the portico where a bed was suspended from the ceiling with gold chains. He lowered her and it swung slightly underneath them.

"I've never been in a bed outside." Maria lay back and spread her legs slightly. She crooked her finger and gestured for him to join her.

"I want to just look at you for a moment." He closed his fingers around his cock and stroked.

"Denton..."

"Shh." He reached out and glided his hand over her body. Her skin was like silk. He cupped one of her breasts, pinching the puckered nipple between his thumb and forefinger. She twisted under his teasing, and when he released the bud, she whimpered.

"Shh. I'm on a mission. Just lie there." Beads of water greeted his hand as he brushed over her abdomen, pausing to separate slender legs so her pink slit was visible. Fire scorched him. It required all of his self-control not to just take her fast and quick. He wanted it to last and ran his hand over the lips of her pussy, enjoying the way her juices clung to his fingers. "You have the prettiest pussy I've ever seen." He leaned down to touch his tongue to the fleshy mounds. They gave under his teasing and he sucked one into his mouth, rolling his tongue around it. She moaned. The taste of her pussy incited him. Almost overpowered by the need to claim her, Denton resisted and took it slow. Pressing his tongue into her opening, he enjoyed the way she responded to each touch. At that moment he cared about only one thing—making love to his wife. His wife. The words excited him and filled him with a sense of protection. He wanted to completely possess her, but it wasn't time. Not yet. Right now he just needed to fuck her until they were both too exhausted to think.

He flicked his tongue over her swollen clit and she moaned, writhing under him. Using his other hand this time, he inserted two fingers into her opening and crooked them until he found the fleshy mound of her pelvis.

The sharp intake of her breath assured him it was her special spot. He wanted to tease her slowly until she couldn't take any more pleasure. Then he'd take her. Hard and fast. He massaged the inside walls of her pussy while licking her clit. She responded and he sensed she wanted more, but purposefully slowed his movements, driving her to thrust her pelvis in an effort to draw him into a faster rhythm.

At length he relented and flicked his tongue faster over the swollen bundle of nerve endings. She ran her hands through his hair, thrusting her hips in time with each stroke. The need to take her set him on fire. He quickened the movements, plunging his fingers in and out of her pussy. He sensed the heat growing in her until strong muscles clamped around his fingers and a burst of hot liquid rushed past them, drenching and soaking his hand. She rocked under the spasms.

All of his self-promises to take it slow incinerated. He lapped up her cum and a deep groan vibrated in his throat. He kissed the lips of her pussy and pulled his fingers from her. Glancing down at her, he met the satisfied look clouding her eyes while he licked her juices from his fingers.

"You taste so sweet." He moved to close his fingers around his cock. "I want to fuck you, Maria." He stroked his erection and envisioned plunging his dick into her channel.

Hooded eyes slit open and a satisfied smile parted her lips. He must have her now! The cum rushed to the tip of his dick. She'd be tight from the orgasm, but he couldn't resist her any longer.

"Take me," she whispered.

He spread her legs wider and eased between them, groaning when he met the wet heat of her pussy. His cock scraped past her silken folds. He paused. The walls of her pussy gripped him and intense sensations pulsed to the sensitized end of his shaft. He pushed a little deeper. Inch by inch, he filled her. He supported himself with his hands firmly planted on either side of her head. His cock throbbed. Her tightened muscles threatened his composure. He was going to lose it unless she relaxed around him. He sunk his cock so deep, he couldn't go any farther. He fit into her all the way to his root. At last he was joined to her as closely as he could and yet it wasn't close enough to sate the sexual hunger driving him for more. Her pussy clenched around his cock and he gritted his teeth, trying to resist the orgasm teasing his senses.

Her legs came up around his waist, and when she locked her feet behind his back to thrust her hips—gods and goddesses, it was almost impossible to hold on to the last threads of control.

Her hands closed around his buttocks and she pressed him harder against her. Wildfire seized Denton. He was like an animal in heat. He thrust his cock in and out of her pussy. Faster and faster. Plunging deeper each time. He wanted to plant his seed. A primal instinct emerged. He must leave his mark inside her. Something all would recognize as his claim on her. Sweat popped out along his spine and rolled down his back. He growled and rammed his cock into her. The small intake of her breath each time he thrust deeper incited him into a frenzied need.

Energy rushed up his cock and cum burst free, exploding inside her. He groaned and continued to rut against her, enjoying the pulsations left in the wake of his release.

"Maria," he breathed. "You...are...mine."

* * * * *

"I'm tired. I think I'll go inside...to bed. Want to join me?" Maria asked, standing on the first step of the underwater staircase.

Denton couldn't stop the smile from spreading over his lips. Her supple body was wet and she glistened like a sea nymph emerging from the ocean. Her curves were perfection. He just wanted to stay there and let his gaze drink in her beauty.

"Denton?" she asked.

He snapped out of the reverie and started across the pool toward her. They'd awakened and decided a dip in the pool was what they needed. But now he needed her. His body ached for her like it was going through withdrawal.

"Food," he said, unable to form a complete sentence. He cleared his throat. They must keep up their strength if they were going to make love again. "Shall I fix us something to snack on?" He reached for her but she squealed and bounded up the steps. He watched in fascination as the water dripped in rivulets around her buttocks.

"The only thing I want to snack on is you." She flashed a teasing smile then darted through the open doorway, leaving behind a wet trail.

"I'm going to get you, Maria Prescott, and when I do, I'll show no mercy."

Her giggles echoed from inside the house. Excitement coursed through Denton and he took the pool steps two at a time. The water flooded away from him and he grabbed a towel from the lounger. Taking long strides, he dried his chest and entered the house. He paused in the doorway to glance back at the ocean. The morning sun radiated over the horizon.

Sunrise.

His breathing sharpened. How quickly life had changed. Chaste had made his life a living hell, and Maria had saved him from it. As he toweled his hair dry, the image of Maria's perfect round ass exposed above the water flashed across his mind. His cock was so hard it pulled his balls tight against him. Damn, he couldn't wait to sink his dick deep inside her sweet little cunt one more time.

He tossed the towel onto a nearby chair and started across the den, leaving puddles of water in his wake. A driving musical beat interrupted his thoughts. It sounded again. He padded over to the sideboard and picked up the crystal globe.

Chaste's name rolled across the quartz surface and he dropped the magic orb back onto its stand. Why couldn't she leave him alone? Was his exile to this island not enough for her? She would not ruin his honeymoon. He gritted his teeth together and opened a drawer, dropping the orb inside and slamming it shut.

How could he have been blind to Chaste's true nature until it was too late? It was better to believe it was part of fate's plan to reunite him with Maria than to admit he'd simply been fooled. Denton's mind raced and he ran his hand through his hair. It was hard to fathom how one fucking mistake could have such irreversible repercussions.

"Denton?" Maria's husky voice interrupted his thoughts. Again he was reminded how ill-fortune had transformed into the best thing to happen to him. With Maria by his side he could survive in this exile.

"You better be in bed," he said, trying to shove the anger from him along with all thoughts of Chaste, her magic spells and her need for revenge.

He took a deep breath, mentally shrugged off the niggling concern that somehow Chaste would harm Maria once news of their marriage reached her. Even Chaste could not gain access to the island. He unclenched his teeth. Maria would remain safe. Right now, he was going to make love to his wife again and enjoy holding her in his arms all day.

"Denton? I'm lonely," Maria cried in a deep sultry voice.

His heartbeat raced. Maria was his. Nothing could come between them, especially Chaste.

Chapter Four

ଚ୨

"Am I dreaming, Denton?" Maria asked, pressing her lips against his neck, wondering about her mission to save him. There didn't seem to be any danger surrounding him.

"If you're dreaming, I hope you never wake up." He rolled onto his back, taking her with him.

She sat up and straddled him, guiding his engorged cock inside her opening. Their bodies were still wet from the dip in the pool and she loved how it felt easing him deeper inside her. His thickness filled her and she rolled her hips, relaxing her muscles around his cock. He ground his hips into her and the rest of his length pressed inside her.

"We're going to have a very happy life together." He cupped her breasts in his hands while she rode him. Slow. Lazy. A rhythm she shared with the sultry breeze.

Denton surprised her when he sat up and buried his head between her breasts, licking and sucking her nipples. Her breath rushed between her lips when quicksilver streaks raced to her pussy.

"I think I'm going to enjoy being married to you," she whispered so softly, she doubted he heard the soft words. She arched her back, letting her head fall backward.

Her pulse throbbed when he caught her hair in his hands and threaded his fingers through her tresses. He leaned in to kiss her neck and slowly released her hair to trail featherlike circles down her back.

She loved the way he touched her. How his large hands felt so warm against her flesh. He dipped them down her back and cupped her buttocks, lifting her forward so her hips tilted up. Her breath caught in her throat with the sensation of his forefinger easing past her buttocks to tease the opening of her anus. He pressed his fingertip into her anus and nerve endings tingled under the pressure.

"Your ass is just as tight as your sweet cunt," he said.

Sharp pulses throbbed to her clit. He ground his cock into her and each time she leaned forward he pressed his finger a little deeper. Electric pulses rushed to her clit. He wiggled his finger, heightening her pleasure so much she was only aware of the cascade of sensations rushing to her pussy. She ground into him, panting.

"Oh, Denton," she breathed. "Oh...it feels so good." She ran her tongue over her lower lip, lifting with each new surge of sexual energy. It undulated up her spine, rising higher and higher until it burst free. Trembling, she gasped and a wave of release spasmed in her. She tightened her muscles around his finger and quickened her movement, sensing he balanced on the edge of orgasm.

Denton felt her come and slowly eased his finger from her opening. She quickened her movements and the tightening of her pussy sent him to the edge of orgasm. He resisted, enjoying the powerful sensations, wanting to savor their lovemaking a little longer. She thrust her hips forward and the crown of his cock tingled. The cum pooled in a rush of heat and burst free. He tensed his body as the spasms shook him.

"Oh gods! Maria!" he panted. The linens were drenched with sweat. The overhead ceiling fan did little to cool the inferno he'd just released.

Maria still straddled him, massaging his chest muscles while rocking in a sensual sway.

"I've never had sex so much in my life," she whispered and traced the length of his nose with her forefinger.

"Is that a complaint?" he chuckled.

"Only that I want more."

Her firm breasts moved each time she rocked forward, taunting him until he reached out to touch them. His fingertips grazed a nipple as she undulated and swayed. The feel of her tender flesh against his fingers left him wanting more. His cock throbbed. If she kept grinding her sweet ass like that he might just get another hard-on and surprise her. As though on cue, a twinge of renewed excitement rushed down his dick, leaving him stiff in its wake.

Growling, he sat up, easing from her and rolled over, taking her with him so she now lay beneath him.

"Oh, Denton," she panted. "You're so strong and sexy. I love it when you get all gargoyle on me. Your excitement makes me weak." Her voice was sultry deep.

"You make me so damn hot," he said and smothered her next words with a deep kiss. Her lips parted and his heart hammered in his chest. He quickly found her tongue, enjoying how it felt to entwine his around hers. She intoxicated him. Her taste was sweet and fiery. He felt like a wild man, imbued with an urgent need to take her again.

He ran his hand down her side, dipping at her waist and curving over the flare of her hip. He groaned. Her skin was as soft as silk. She was pliable beneath his touch. Soft where he was hard. Denton shifted so he could separate her legs, and when he slid his hand between her thighs, her breath came in hard puffs through her nostrils.

He broke from the kiss and she panted, her breasts rising and falling with each labored breath.

"I'm going to sink my cock deep into your tight little pussy and make you come so hard," he breathed and trailed his hand to her pussy, slipping his finger between the two mounds to the tender spot. She lifted her hips and moaned. He rubbed his finger over her swollen clit, stroking and teasing until she was writhing and thrashing beneath his touch.

He couldn't wait any longer and guided himself into her opening. He pressed past the wet heat and groaned under the tightness that greeted his entry. The walls of her pussy squeezed around his cock and he ground into her until she'd taken him completely.

The image of her ass tilted above the pool's surface flashed across his mind and he rammed his cock in and out of her pussy. Fucking her stimulated his deepest instincts. He was driven to ravish her. All of her. Completely. And he did. He lifted her legs and kissed her thigh, rolling his tongue against her skin as though he was kissing her pussy. He quickened his movements and pounded his cock into her. Fire licked his nerve endings and he growled between clenched teeth. The energy carried him faster to the height of pleasure. His cock scraped in and out of her channel until the fire screamed through him. He stiffened. His muscles tensed and his seed erupted from his cock, bursting inside her. Panting, he bowed his head and leaned over her.

"I love you," he breathed, still burning for her. Still unsated in his hunger to claim her. There was plenty of time to perform the ritual mating with her. He must wait until she was ready, and when she was, they would have the most glorious gargoyle sex.

* * * * *

Music drifted through the room and Maria pulled from the dredges of sleep, blinking in the dim light. Yawning, she lifted from the bed. What was that? It sounded again and she recognized it as the messaging of a crystal ball. Grabbing the displaced blanket from the edge of the bed, she wrapped it around her and followed the muffled sound down the hall into the den.

The room was dark but a blue light glowed around the edges of a drawer in the sideboard. Why was his messenger in a drawer? And who would be summoning Denton at this time of night? She walked over to the table and opened the drawer, reaching for the orb. Her fingers closed around it just as a name scrolled over the globe.

"Chaste?" She tried to release the ball but was too late. She'd accidentally pressed the button and answered the summons. A blonde woman's face curled over the ball.

"Denton? Are you there? Turn on a light, will you? I can't see you." The porcelain face hardened into a frown.

Maria's pulse quickened and she clenched her jaw at the possessive tone in the woman's voice. Just who was this woman? She'd not thought about Denton's love life before her. Perhaps this was a girlfriend.

"Okay. I don't need to see you. You know why I'm crystalling you. It's been a year, surely you aren't still angry. I'm tired of waiting, Denton. I still want... Well, you know what I want, don't you, baby? That special magic only you can give to me. I'll be there tomorrow night. Understand? I want what's mine."

"Maria?" Denton called from the bedroom.

She tapped the orb, breaking off the connection. She stiffened her spine. Denton could deal with Chaste tomorrow. Tonight was their honeymoon and no ex-girlfriend was going to interfere with their bliss. She hurried back to the bedroom just as he was getting up.

"Sorry," she smiled.

"Baby? Where'd you go? I have a difficult time keeping you in my bed. I hope this isn't going to be a habit." He lay back down.

"I couldn't sleep."

"What's wrong?" he asked, tossing back the covers so she could climb in.

"Nothing." She slid back into bed. "I just woke up."

His arms engulfed her and all thoughts of Chaste fell away. He lowered his head and captured one of her nipples between his lips. Her breath latched in her throat and she closed her eyes, enjoying the sensations he brought to her. Large hands moved over her body, massaging, probing. He cupped her buttocks and released her nipples. Wet and sensitized. Aching for more.

He trailed a series of short kisses down and over her abdomen. She rolled onto her knees and straddled him. His deep groan sent tendrils of excitement curling down her spine. Grasping her ass, he planted his head between her legs. She spread her legs to afford him better access to her pussy and rolled her hips to meet his touch. His tongue twisted around the outer lips of her pussy, darting in and out, teasing the rim of her channel. When his fingers began to toy with her clit, she leaned back on her hands and arched to his strokes. His other hand slid between her buttocks, pressing firmly into her anus.

It felt as though her blood was a molten flow of fire. Her pulse throbbed in her ears. Wave after wave of sensation seized her and her body shuddered in sweet release.

"I'm in pleasure paradise," she breathed.

* * * * *

"Stop calling me, Chaste." Denton's voice echoed from the den and Maria threw back the covers. Padding down the hall, she recognized the irritation in his tone.

"The Coalition granted me permission, Denton. I'm coming to the island. I'll be there at sunset. You better be prepared to give me what I want." The familiar female voice grated.

Maria released a deep sigh.

"Maria, baby." Denton spun around to face her, dropping the crystal ball onto the table. "I can explain." The pounding surf beyond the open patio door matched the drumming of her heart.

"I understand you knew her before me, Denton. She's not a threat to me, if that's what you're worried about. If she becomes a problem you can just call the Guard—"

"Stop. Please. You know it doesn't work that way here." He ran his hand through his hair. Bright sunlight shone through the windows onto him.

"You didn't transform into stone again when the sun hit you. How is that?"

"We've been through this, Maria. I'm not a gargoyle here. Remember?"

"No. I told you I don't remember everything. I don't understand why you aren't a gargoyle. And who is Chaste and what's this Coalition she mentioned?"

"Seriously?" He glanced up at her. "You don't remember being taken before them?"

She shook her head.

"Okay. Look. Chaste is the reason I'm here. Just like someone is the reason you're here."

"The person responsible for me being here is not some evil bitch."

He frowned at her.

"Okay, if you don't turn to stone on this magical island, then why don't we fly around for a while and discuss this later?"

"Fly?" His laughter was harsh. Empty. "Who the hell can fly anymore? Our magic was stripped from us long before we ever stepped foot on this island. We're prisoners, Maria. How can you forget that?"

"W-What?" She stumbled backward and sat down on the couch. Was it true? Was that why she was unable to release her wings? She'd thought it was from being intoxicated. She shook her head. "Just where are we?"

"You don't recall being sentenced to this prison."

"Sentenced?" She shook her head.

"The only way to get here is to be convicted of a crime."

"The Dreamland Government would never sentence its most glorious hero to prison, Denton."

"They sure as hell did, baby." He held his arms out to his sides. "Here I stand. It was all over the news. You couldn't miss it."

"Well...I've been away." Her mind raced. Had her powers really been stripped without her knowing it? "Seriously, Denton, I wasn't convicted of anything. We have to find a way off this island and exonerate you."

"Exonerate?" He stopped pacing. Tenderness softened his scowl. "You didn't ask why I was here or what I did. You just assume I'm innocent."

"Well of course you're innocent, silly." She stood to encircle her arms around his neck. "The first thing we have to do is find a way off this island."

"Impossible. The Wizard Coalition maintains a fortified spell over the entire island that prevents anyone from leaving. Now if I still had my magic, sure, I could leave, but..." He turned from her and resumed pacing. "Chaste will be here at sunset. She wears the amulet that holds my powers captive. Just like whoever sent you here now holds your powers," he stopped pacing, "unless you gave up your magic. They didn't torture you like they did me, did they, baby?" He gripped her upper arms. "Tell me they didn't. I couldn't stand it if they did."

"No. They tortured you?" Pain pierced her heart.

"Yeah, the bastards tried to force me to relinquish my magic to the Coalition. Dammit! They have no right to force us to give our magic to them. It's supposed to be suspended in the amulet for the duration of the sentence. If I ever get off this island, I'm going to bring them down. I'm going to expose their corrupt enterprise. But I swear by all my ancestors if Chaste thinks I'll buckle under her threats when I wouldn't under the Wizards'—" He snorted and raked his hand through his hair.

"Slow down, Denton. How does Chaste have your magic?"

"As the victim of my supposed crime, Chaste was granted keeper of my powers that are trapped within the amethyst amulet she wears around her neck."

"Just what was your crime?"

"Rejecting her affections," he jeered and then shook his head. "She framed me for her brother's murder."

"Oh sweet fairy dust." Her knees weakened and she gripped the back of a nearby chair.

"They were always in a power struggle for the family fortune, so she killed him and framed me."

"That witch! You may be powerless, but I'm not. I'm a Hussy Warrior Hunter and I've been trained for this. Don't you see? I was sent here to rescue you, Denton. My teacher, Danu, placed me on the island."

"Baby, you're still in a partial fog. No one has stronger magic than the Wizard Coalition."

"I daresay Danu could mop the floor with the Coalition." She folded her arms over her chest. "So how does it all work? How does someone relinquish their magic?"

"By exerting free will to bequeath your power to the keeper of the amulet. I won't ever give Chaste my magic."

"Why does she want your magic?" Maria asked. "What will she do with a warrior's magic?"

"She's involved with the Coalition. They have too much control for a private concern contracted to oversee the island penal system."

"But what do they intend to use all this magic for? Some of it cannot be of value to them, like troll energy unless they are opening a mine."

"Chaste let it slip last time I saw her. With enough magic, the Coalition can overthrow the Dreamland world government." He frowned. "I try not to think about it since I'm helpless to stop them."

"But if you were free, you could stop them." Her mind raced. This must be why Denton was so important and why she'd been sent to rescue him. She touched his arm, feeling his pain. "How does the Coalition prevent prisoners who've served their time and are released from telling the world what is going on here?"

His laughter was brittle, sending an icy chill down her back. "No one leaves here, Maria. Don't you get it? They can't risk it. All prisoners scheduled for release either die in a freak accident, succumb to a sudden illness or refuse to reclaim their magic and shift into the human world."

"Surely when none of the prisoners return to Dreamland it causes suspicions. Their families—"

"Are you serious? Those on the outside don't care what happens to us. Families are ashamed. There is no redemption or forgiveness. If we were to return, we'd be shunned for the rest of our lives. And no one would ever believe a condemned, even an ex."

"That's not right. Oh, Denton, if they get your magic, then they'll have the most powerful of all gargoyle magic. No army will be able to stop them."

His face darkened. "I don't know how I can stop them, Maria. As long as Chaste wears the amulet, I can't touch it. And without my magic, I remain a mortal man trapped on this island prison."

Why hadn't Danu just told her straight out she'd be fighting an evil wizard spawn? Perhaps the seer didn't know every aspect of the mission. Maybe Danu's job was just to prepare her for any kind of situation. And she had.

"You'll be whole again very soon. I promise. I'll return your magic to you."

"You need to sit down." He gently pressed her onto the couch. "Look, baby," he kneeled on one knee in front of her, "I'm really moved that you're ready to fight for me, but you don't have magical powers anymore. I can't protect you. They stole my gargoyle essence—" His voice choked off and he lifted his hand to stroke her cheek. Whenever he touched her, there was only one thing Maria wanted to do and right now she needed to think. She grasped his hand and held it to her breasts.

"Don't you see? I was sent to save you. You're the warrior."

"Oh baby, you aren't thinking straight because of the tequila hangover." He smoothed her hair.

"Dammit!" Maria jumped up and willed her wings to release. They popped out of her back and she fluttered them, lifting off the floor toward the ceiling.

"What the hell?" Denton watched his wife fly around the room. Her gold and purple wings quivered so fast he could barely distinguish the jewel-like quality of their pattern.

"See? I'm telling you the truth. I'm not a prisoner here."

"Maria," he laughed and reached for her when she zoomed past. "Okay. I believe you."

Hope sparked to life once more. It was miraculous watching her in such magical glory. Real magic. He thought he'd never witness magic again.

"We can beat Chaste at her own game." Maria winked at him. "Faeries have a few secret talents."

"I've benefited from many of them." Love swelled in him.

"But you've not seen this." She lifted her arms above her head and vanished.

"Maria!" Denton spun around. Was she just moving too fast for him to see or had she really disappeared?

"I'm right here." Her warm breath brushed over his ear. The air stirred cooler beside him and he knew she'd left.

He jerked around and felt her breast against his arm.

"How did you do that?" He reached out to enfold her in his arms.

"Faerie magic, my love." She rematerialized and he brushed his lips against hers.

"When I first saw you on the beach, I was so overcome with joy that I wouldn't allow myself to ask you how you came to be in this forsaken place." Guilt crashed around him. "I was selfish. I didn't want anything other than the spark of happiness you gave me to exist between us—"

"Shh." She pressed her fingers over his lips. "It's okay, Denton. I understand. You don't need to explain." She stroked his face and he tightened his arms around her.

"But I want to explain. You've saved me, Maria. Your love brought me back to life and showed me that any place could be paradise as long as I'm with you. I apologize, my love. For not pressing you that one time I did ask about your circumstances. I assumed you'd been accused of a crime and imprisoned just like I had. I should have asked again. Shown how much I care about what happened to you, because I do."

"Shh." She covered his lips with hers in a short kiss. "You've shown me how much you care, Denton. And we'd have talked…in time." She blushed.

He pressed her head to his chest and buried his face into silky dark tresses, soaking in the sweet aroma through his nostrils. Instantly lost in the quickening pulses rushing to his dick, he wanted to be inside her and feel her writhing under him. The ache to feel her body spasm as he pleasured her consumed him.

"Enough talk," she said and pushed him onto the couch, diving on top of him. Laughter filled the den and Denton knew together they could defeat any foe, especially Chaste.

Chapter Five

"Let's not waste time with pleasantries. Give me your magic." The woman's seductive tone mocked her words. Maria's instincts went into overdrive. Anger bristled over her.

Maria smoothed back her hair and hurried from the bedroom before Chaste pushed Denton too far and their chance to implement the plan was ruined. She evoked the shield of invisibility and burst into the room. Denton stood across from a tall blonde. The woman was dressed in a black mini-dress that revealed her most prominent feature—endless, slender legs. She appeared to be in her twenties, even though she sounded much older.

"Are you so naïve to think you can beat me? The Coalition?"

"It's time for you to leave before I do something you and the Coalition will regret."

Chaste laughed. "Oh I think not." She turned for the open patio door. "Raphael?"

A large man dressed in black appeared on the portico but remained outside as though standing guard.

"See, lover?" Chaste purred and flipped her long tresses over her shoulder. "And I have more where he came from just waiting off shore. All it takes is one word from me. So we're just going to make ourselves comfy while we wait for the Coalition to arrive. Oh, did I neglect to mention they're paying you a personal visit tonight? They're anxious to have done with all this nasty business. I've been awarded your magic permanently."

Denton felt the air stir around him and knew Maria was positioning herself. His heart slammed against his chest wall. Soon he would be gargoyle again. Adrenaline pumped through him.

"While transferring your magic to the amulet was easy and done with a simple touch while I wore it, unfortunately, it's not doing me any good like this. So you need to relinquish it to me, love."

"Don't you enjoy wearing it around your scrawny neck?" His fingers itched to close around her long neck.

"I know what you're thinking. Even if you managed to remove it from me, it would set you on fire. Just say you relinquish your free will and poof, I'll be gone. Your magic becomes mine." She rubbed against Denton and he tensed. When she draped her arms over his shoulders and ran her hand up his neck, it was all he could do not to shove her away.

"What will you do with the amulet once you force me to grant you the use of my magic?"

"Why do you care?"

"It serves as the conduit for my powers. If it fell into the wrong hands—"

"Once I have your magic, no one else can claim it. I guess *you* could reclaim it, but that's not going to happen."

"So had I been wearing it, I could have taken your powers?"

"Hmm." She ran her tongue over glossy lips.

The air stirred around him.

"Don't make her angry," Maria whispered in his ear.

"You're so brilliant, my sexy gargoyle." Chaste pressed against him, grinding her hips into his. "I think once you relinquish your powers to me I'll keep the amulet as a souvenir."

"Gargoyle magic is very different from witch energy."

"I'm only half-witch. The wizard in me will know how to tame it."

He laughed.

"You think your essence can't be tamed?"

"Not by you."

"Kiss her." Maria's lips pressed against his ear. "Kiss her."

"I might just prove you wrong once the Coalition's business is done."

"You can try, but remember I've already sampled everything you have."

"Why, you bastard!" Chaste shoved from him.

"Dammit, Denton, kiss her and I'll unclasp her necklace," Maria whispered.

Bile churned in his stomach at the thought of touching Chaste, but he reached out and closed his fingers around her wrist. She cried out in surprise and then giggled.

"Why, Denton." She turned around.

He jerked her to him, trapping her slender arms by her sides.

"You still have some fire left as a mere mortal," Chaste panted, struggling to free herself yet seeming to enjoy being helpless. "Maybe I'll keep you as a plaything."

Denton leaned in to kiss her but she stiffened.

"No!" Her eyes widened on him. "The amulet!"

Denton dropped his gaze to her chest. The chain went limp and the amulet slid down her cleavage.

"What are you doing? How? How did you get magic?"

The chain lifted between them and draped around Denton's neck. The moment the amethyst touched his skin it began to glow.

"You can't have that. It's mine!"

He released Chaste. She reached out and grabbed the amulet, trying to lift it from his chest. Her scream pierced his ears. She dropped it and clutched her burned hand to her chest.

"I reclaim my magic. It belongs to me," Denton shouted.

A brilliant light burst from the amulet and a wave of electricity sparked through him in a mixture of pain and pleasure. He tensed his muscles against the power roiling inside him.

"You can't reclaim your gargoyle magic. It belongs to me!" Chaste started for him, but Maria materialized in front of him. Denton tried to straighten, but pain brought him to his knees.

"Who the hell are you? How did you..." Chaste sniffed, tilting her head. "You're a fucking fae?" Confusion vexed Chaste's face and her gaze flashed from Maria back to him.

"You won't do any more harm against Denton," Maria said in a tone he'd never heard before. It was the voice of a powerful warrior. He tried to stand, but the transferring power kept him on one knee.

Chaste lifted her hand and a wave of energy rippled across the room. Denton called out to Maria as it blasted toward her. With both arms folded together in front of her, Maria shielded herself. A crystalline bubble encapsulated her. Denton had never seen anything like it. She really did have secret talents.

"You bitch!" Chaste screamed and swung her arm back. A ball of fire flashed in her open palm and she hurled it toward Maria. The fire hit the shield surrounding Maria and ricocheted back toward Chaste who ducked as it whizzed just inches from her head. The blazing ball crashed through the window and struck the guard outside. His clothes ignited and he yelled, diving into the pool.

Denton tried to stand once more, but it was as though he'd turned to stone. He didn't recall experiencing pain when

Chaste had stolen his magic. How long did restoration take? He needed to help Maria. He stopped struggling. Perhaps his resistance was the reason for the pain. He'd not suspected Chaste was stealing his magic in the courtroom and hadn't felt a thing. He relaxed his muscles, willing his body to accept the pain and let it consume him.

"Denton? Are you all right?" Maria asked and took a step closer to him. The shield surrounding her moved with her as though part of her.

"Stay away from him. His magic belongs to me. I have legal custody of it."

"You manipulated the courts to do your bidding. You don't own any part of Denton. He's a gargoyle! You know what that means in our world, don't you? A mighty warrior. How dare you do this to one so full of honor and decency. You're a corrupt creature, Chaste. I warn you now. You will pay for what you've done."

Denton smiled up at his wife. So brave and full of fire. She leaned over him and the shield protecting her expanded around him.

"I don't know who you think you are, little faerie, but you can't run away from legal justice."

"I'm Denton's wife." Maria paused in helping him stand. "And if you think you can threaten us then you don't understand the magic of true love. As for the legal aspects of my husband being here, I have a few connections within Dreamland Government and I'm sure once they hear his story, justice will indeed be served." She turned back to Denton and supported him so he could straighten.

"Come, my love, we're flying out of here."

At that moment, the love and gratitude he felt for her burst inside him. Maria had restored him. She loved him, whether he was gargoyle or manflesh. At that moment he vowed to do everything in his power to deserve such unconditional love.

His attention snapped back to Chaste as she rushed for them, screaming and sobbing. Maria whispered something in fae language. Chaste jumped for them, but when she struck the energy bubble, she was repelled. The force threw her back and she crashed into the opposite wall. Her limp body slumped to the floor. Denton floated with Maria through the open patio doors and above the pool. Chaste's pitiful wailing was drowned out by the ocean's roar.

"Say goodbye to your prison, my love." Maria hugged his arm to her chest.

"I say goodbye to our love nest and look forward to creating a new one with you." He smiled down at her.

The sensation of his wings releasing through the slits in his back felt strange and yet it was as if his magic had never left him. Denton spread the feathers apart and moved his wings up and down.

"Flight," he sighed. "I thought I'd never feel my wings again. Thank you, Maria." Tears welled in his eyes and he looked away.

"It's my deepest pleasure." She squeezed his hand. The protection bubble disappeared and they flew side by side into the night sky, away from the island.

Damn, it felt good to be a gargoyle again. His body shook under the return of his gargoyle essence. The raw power of magic once more pumped through his veins. He was complete. "We have to find a safe place to hide. We'll need time to launch our defense for breaking me out of prison and proving I was framed," he said.

"I know just the place," she smiled.

Denton wanted to burn the image of her silhouette against the moon into his mind, forever. His wife. His rescuer. His beloved.

* * * * *

"I'm surprised how quickly the Dreamland Executive Committee returned their verdict," Denton said, nuzzling her neck.

Delightful shivers raced over Maria.

"You were incredible on the stand today. Your testimony exonerated me." Denton tugged her closer.

"You were innocent. It was easy for the High Judges to see the truth once it was placed in front of them."

"It wasn't such an easy feat. Give yourself credit. Without Chaste being there to question, it required great skill to convince them."

"They know you, Denton. Your deeds. Your past spoke in your defense. There was no logical reason for you to kill Chaste's brother. Once the Wizard Coalition's practice of stealing magic from their prisoners was exposed, it became clear they had framed you. I enjoyed watching their evil empire unravel before the world. It'll be a long process sorting through all of the cases to determine who was unjustly incarcerated like you."

"You saved me, Maria." His lips touched her cheek and she melted against him.

"All in a day's work for a Hussy," she sighed, enjoying the way it felt being naked in the tub with him. Rose petals floated on top of the bath water. Her breasts buoyed in the bath.

"I'm also impressed with your connections within the world government. You made it happen so quickly. Typically we'd have months, even years to await a hearing."

"Thank my father the next time you see him."

"Having a father-in-law as the newly appointed Fae Chancellor was—"

"Luck?" She stared up at him and fell silent. So many emotions were conveyed in those blue depths. Her pulse quickened. "So when do you report for duty?" she asked, sad that he would be leaving but happy he'd been reinstated in the

Elite Guard. It was part of who he was and why she loved him so much.

"Not for another week."

"Hmm..." She rested her head against his shoulder. "I wonder what we can do between now and then?" She turned in the deep tub and reached out to close her fingers around his cock.

"I can think of a few things." His breath fanned over her cheek. "That feels nice."

She stroked up and down, enjoying the way he felt beneath her massaging fingers.

"Now you've done it." He covered her mouth with his. Excitement surged in her when he tightened his arms around her. Thrusting her tongue into his mouth, she tried to capture his tongue. He met her aggressive moves and she knew he was restraining the fervor pumping in him.

She broke from his kiss, gasping for air, and before she knew what was happening found herself being lifted from the water and laid down onto the large towels along the edge of the Roman tub. He joined her and she quickly regained control by straddling him.

She leaned forward and brought her lips around his cock, taking him into her mouth while twirling her tongue over the crown. Slowly, she pulled him from her mouth and then took him inside her mouth once more.

"Oh baby," he groaned, reaching out to caress her hair. "I want to take you like a gargoyle."

She paused and released his cock. She held him between her hands and stroked his cock, enjoying the way he felt. How the tiny bead of cum seeped past the pink slit. She rubbed it over his skin.

"What's gargoyle sex? Isn't that what we've been having?"

"Mating for gargoyles is special. We can only do it one time. We must perform a ritual of anal sex but only after we've proclaimed our mate."

"So that's what having gargoyle sex means." She paused to look at him. "Anal sex? All this time I thought it meant really powerful sex."

He sat up and she moved to kiss him.

"Well, it is," he spoke between kisses. "I've never known anyone I wanted to mate. You are the only one for me, Maria."

"Oh, Denton. Of course I want to be your mate, only...I must admit, your cock is just so big—"

"You forget gargoyles have magic too."

Excitement and a sense of the taboo sent quickening pulses to her pussy.

"I can enter much smaller than I am."

"You can?"

He nodded and she bit her lower lip.

"I can't increase my natural size, but I can become smaller. It's part of the pleasure of being a gargoyle. You'll enjoy it. I promise." He cupped her face in his hands. "Maria, I claim you as my eternal mate." He kissed her. It was a tender kiss. Slow.

Warm hands moved over her, gliding against her skin still wet from their bath. She closed her eyes and relaxed under his touch. She would let him guide her. His hand slid between her legs and teased the outer lips of her pussy. She was instantly lost in the excited teasing.

A low growl vibrated in his throat. Primal. Possessive. Each breath came faster than the last and Maria sensed a difference in his lovemaking. She didn't know how it was possible, but he was somehow sexier, even more desirable. Perhaps it was because he was now his true self.

He encouraged her to turn over onto her stomach and she lifted to her knees, tilting her ass. He clasped her hips and tugged her to him. The feel of his cock, hard and hot, when he pressed it between her buttocks, set her blood on fire. The lubricant was cool and provided a sharp contrast to the thick heat entering her anus. He filled her and she leaned forward in reflex as he penetrated the first inch then the next. Delightful sensations cascaded over her.

She was surprised when his hand slipped around her waist and firm fingers separated her labia. She panted when he stroked her clit, slowly at first while he inched his cock deeper inside her.

Moving under the growing heat, Maria relaxed her muscles to accept him as his cock expanded inside her. Each stroke of his fingers sent electric pulses surging through her. The pressure of his cock intensified the sensations. Her senses were electrified. She'd never known such pleasure. She leaned her head down, letting her hair tumble to the mattress.

He quickened his strokes and she moved against his fingertips, hot against her clit. Teasing energy snaked around her spine, lifting and tempting her to the edge of orgasm. She ached for release but wanted the pleasure to last. She ran her tongue over her lips and imagined licking his thick cock. He groaned and eased slightly from her. The movement charged her nerve endings. Delightful tingles rushed over her and there was no stopping the sudden rush of energy. It raced up her spine and exploded in a powerful orgasm. She throbbed. Every sensory point in her body twinged and she was seized by spasms.

He leaned forward, kissing her shoulder. His heated breath fanned over her and she knew he restrained himself from taking her hard. His body tensed and his cock throbbed inside her. His hot cum filled her.

"Now you are my true mate," he whispered, twirling his tongue around the rim of her ear.

Maria had never felt so complete. She was his. Denton belonged to her and no one could ever separate them. She'd accomplished her Hussy mission. She smiled, enjoying the way it felt having him buried so deeply inside her. Connected to her as no other ever would.

* * * * *

Maria finished dressing and wondered how long Denton would be at headquarters. She decided to wait for him outside on the terrace overlooking Dream City. The night air greeted her in a rush of heat, the day's heat rising from the gold streets below. She closed her eyes and drew in the fresh scents riding the night wind. Magic pulsed everywhere.

"Hubby not home?" came the feminine voice and Maria's eyes flew open. She spun around to find Chaste standing in the open doorway.

"How did you get in here?" Maria asked, glancing past Chaste to make sure she wasn't accompanied by any bodyguards. "The authorities are looking for you. I suggest you leave."

"I don't think so. We have unfinished business." Chaste took a step closer and Maria braced her feet apart, prepared to fight.

"You got your ass kicked the last time we met, Chaste."

Chaste laughed. "You were lucky, faerie. I came prepared this time with faerie dust." She held out her hand and blew.

Maria tried to evoke protection, but red and gold flecks sparkled in the moonlight and fell over her, zapping the energy from her. She collapsed onto the tile floor.

"See? I can always think faster than you or Denton." Chaste stood over her. "Now we'll wait for lover man to get home."

"This won't change anything, Chaste. Denton is free. You can't hurt him anymore."

"Now see, that's where you're wrong. I can hurt him by hurting you."

"You just won't learn." Denton spoke behind Chaste.

Maria sighed with relief. He folded his wings against his back. Something glinted in his hand and Maria realized it was the amulet. If Chaste was able to wrestle it from him... There was no telling what other magic tricks Chaste possessed. There would be no undoing a second taking of his powers.

"Denton, no!" Maria cried out.

He closed his fingers around the amulet and grabbed Chaste's hand with his free one. She screamed, writhing and pulling against his grip. Maria thought how useless Chaste's magic was against Denton. The wizard-witch no longer had the strength of the Wizard Coalition behind her.

"Your magic is mine," Denton said, and a wave of black and gray energy curled from Chaste's chest. She shrieked. Her eyes widened on the amulet as her magic entered it.

"You can't do this!" she wailed. The last bit of magic left her and she crumpled to the floor, moaning. Denton ran over to Maria and lifted her into his arms.

"I'm okay. She didn't hurt me. The dust doesn't last very long."

"I was so scared for you." He covered her lips with his and she knew he needed reassurance she was whole and unharmed.

She broke from the kiss. "I'm okay, Denton. Really. How did you know she was here?"

"Our mating. We now have a telepathic connection. I heard you call out to me."

"Oh, Denton." She hugged him.

"Even Hussies need rescuing once in a while."

"What shall we do with her?" Maria asked.

"I think we should save the government some trouble and personally see that her sentence is finally carried out. Let's deliver her and the amulet to the island warden."

"I like the way you think. You do the flying. I'm going to be busy teasing you." Maria held her hands in front of her and willed a ball of energy to surround Chaste.

She stepped into Denton's embrace and let him cradle her in his arms. His large gargoyle wings lifted them into the night. Maria motioned for the bubble imprisoning Chaste to follow them.

"I love you, Maria," Denton said. "Once we've delivered Chaste to her new island home, what do you say we finish our honeymoon in the blue mountains of Treastente?"

"Hmm...moonlit skinny dips in the Agate Sea and slow lovemaking on pearl-littered beaches underneath the stars?" she sighed, already feeling the ocean breeze.

"Something like that."

"It sounds like the perfect place to make love to my sexy gargoyle husband, as long as you promise there will also be gargoyle sex."

"Always."

Maria lifted her gaze and met the hunger in his eyes. Her heartbeat quickened. Magic was in the air as they flew toward the island. Danu had neglected to tell her the mission's ultimate reward would be her secret dream coming true. Denton.

The End

Also by Nathalie Gray

ℰꙅ

eBooks:

Acid Rayne *(with Ciana Stone)*

Bain's Wolf

DamNATION

Femme Metal 1: Femme Metal

Femme Metal 2: Hot Target

Femme Metal 3: Cold Fusion

Immortalis

Intergalactic Nick

Lycan Warriors 1: Feral

Lycan Warriors 2: Primal

Lycan Warriors 3: Carnal

Lycan Warriors 4: Animal

Mechanical Rose

Shades of Silver

Sinful

Tease

The Hussies 2: Cassiopeia

The Hussies 4: Gladius

Thrill of the Hunt

Timely Defense

Whispering

Wolfsbane

Print Books:

About Nathalie Gray

ഇ

I am a mother, spouse, older sister, writer, ex-soldier, high school drop-out, dog owner (or dog owned), half couch potato/half intermittent jogger, wannabe renovator and avid reader who watches too much television, sinks too much money in clothes, likes animals more than humans, recycles, wore braces, never downloads copyrighted stuff, was a nerd without the grades, has a belly laugh that turns heads in theaters, can't stand bullying, is mother hawk more than mother hen, votes even if candidates aren't that great and thinks formal education is highly overrated (probably because she has none).

Also by Ciana Stone

ಐ

eBooks:

Acid Rayne (*with Nathalie Gray*)
Cougar Challenge: Cam's Holiday
Feels Like the First Time
Hearts of Fire 1: Memory's Eye
Hearts of Fire 5: Entwined Hearts (*with Nicole Austin, TJ Michaels & N.J. Walters*)
Hot in the Saddle 1: Chase 'n' Ana
Hot in the Saddle 2: Molding Clay
Hot in the Saddle 3: Scout 'n' Cole
Hot in the Saddle 4: Conn 'n' Caleb
Redeemed
Riding Ranger
Sequins, Saddles and Spurs 3: Trouble in Chaps
Sexplorations 2: The Thing about Cowboys
Sexplorations 4: Finding Her Rhythm
Sexplorations 6: Working Up a Sweat
The Hussies: Sin in Jeans
Wyatt's Chance

Print Books:

Acid Rayne (*with Nathalie Gray*)
Cougar Challenge: Tease a Cougar (*anthology*)
Hot in the Saddle 1 & 2: Unbridled
Hot in the Saddle 3 & 4: Unrestrained

About Ciana Stone

ဆ

Ciana Stone has been reading since the age of three, and wrote her first story at age five. Since then she enjoyed writing as a solitary form of entertainment, before coming out of the closet to share her stories with others. She holds several post graduate degrees and has often been referred to as a professional student. Her latest fields of interest are quantum mechanics and Taoism. When she is not writing (or studying) she enjoys painting (canvas, not walls), sculpting, running, hiking and yoga. She lives with her longtime lover in several locations in the United States.

About Sally Painter

∞

When an astrologer told Sally, "Beneath that smart business suit you're wearing beats the heart of a Hussy," she was inspired!

Born in the South and into an Irish/Scottish family meant storytelling was a natural part of her life, especially the ghost stories of her state. From an early age she had many encounters with real ghosts and years later was invited to participate in a three-year paranormal project. Sally went on to host a monthly paranormal workshop and paranormal radio talk show.

Nowadays when not writing hot sexy gargoyles, vampires and futuristic hunks, Sally writes about romance at romanceexaminer.com and various topics at lovetoknow.com.

∞

The authors welcome comments from readers. You can find their websites and email addresses on their author bio pages at www.ellorascave.com.

Tell Us What You Think

We appreciate hearing reader opinions about our books. You can email us at Service@ellorascave.com (when contacting Customer Service, be sure to state the book title and author).

Why an electronic book?

We live in the Information Age—an exciting time in the history of human civilization, in which technology rules supreme and continues to progress in leaps and bounds every minute of every day. For a multitude of reasons, more and more avid literary fans are opting to purchase e-books instead of paper books. The question from those not yet initiated into the world of electronic reading is simply: *Why?*

1. *Price.* An electronic title at Ellora's Cave Publishing runs anywhere from 40% to 75% less than the cover price of the exact same title in paperback format. Why? Basic mathematics and cost. It is less expensive to publish an e-book (no paper and printing, no warehousing and shipping) than it is to publish a paperback, so the savings are passed along to the consumer.

2. *Space.* Running out of room in your house for your books? That is one worry you will never have with electronic books. For a low one-time cost, you can purchase a handheld device specifically designed for e-reading. Many e-readers have large, convenient screens for viewing. Better yet, hundreds of titles can be stored within your new library—on a single microchip. There are a variety of e-readers from different manufacturers. You can also read e-books on your PC or laptop computer. (Please note that Ellora's Cave does not endorse any specific brands.

You can check our website at www.ellorascave.com for information we make available to new consumers.)

3. *Mobility.* Because your new e-library consists of only a microchip within a small, easily transportable e-reader, your entire cache of books can be taken with you wherever you go.

4. *Personal Viewing Preferences.* Are the words you are currently reading too small? Too large? Too... ANNOYING? Paperback books cannot be modified according to personal preferences, but e-books can.

5. *Instant Gratification.* Is it the middle of the night and all the bookstores near you are closed? Are you tired of waiting days, sometimes weeks, for bookstores to ship the novels you bought? Ellora's Cave Publishing sells instantaneous downloads twenty-four hours a day, seven days a week, every day of the year. Our webstore is never closed. Our e-book delivery system is 100% automated, meaning your order is filled as soon as you pay for it.

Those are a few of the top reasons why electronic books are replacing paperbacks for many avid readers.

As always, Ellora's Cave welcomes your questions and comments. We invite you to email us at Service@ellorascave.com or write to us directly at Ellora's Cave Publishing Inc., 1056 Home Avenue, Akron, OH 44310-3502.

MAKE EACH DAY MORE EXCITING WITH OUR

ELLORA'S
CAVEMEN
CALENDAR

☥ WWW.ELLORASCAVE.COM ☥

ELLORA'S CAVE
Romanticon

Annual convention
for women who
refuse to behave

Discover for yourself why readers can't get enough of the multiple award-winning publisher Ellora's Cave. Be sure to visit EC on the web at www.ellorascave.com to find erotic reading experiences that will leave you breathless. You can also find our books at all the major e-tailers (Barnes & Noble, Amazon Kindle, Sony, Kobo, Google, Apple iBookstore, All Romance eBooks, and others).

www.ellorascave.com

CPSIA information can be obtained at www.ICGtesting.com
Printed in the USA
LVOW11s1639221213

366449LV00001B/80/P